BLOOD ON BLOOMSDAY

Also by Chris Bieker

Murder at Manito

BLOOD
ON
BLOOMSDAY

A Rex Begonia Mystery

Chris Bieker

Print Edition ISBN: 978-1-7352191-2-7
Digital Edition ISBN: 978-1-7352191-3-4

Printed in the United States of America

For my three mothers:

Rose Bieker, who gave me life and taught me to read.
Mary (Brown) Munoz, my Godmother and pre-school teacher.
Grace Stetzik, my mother-in-law who inspires me to write.

Chapter 1

IT'S PERSONAL

Tuesday Afternoon, Mid April

Detective Rex Begonia slipped into the fifth-floor hospital room. Chief Barney Blueblood's tall, broad back blocked the view of the body in the bed while the scene of the sun setting outside the window caught the detective's eye. A purplish red settled over the plains in the West beyond the downtown as lights began to illuminate the Lilac City. "Chief . . ."

"Rex. Sorry, I didn't see you come in . . ." The Spokane police chief's voice trailed off as he turned to face his top homicide detective, who had hurried to Holy Heart Hospital after receiving an urgent call.

As the chief pivoted, Rex caught a glimpse of what appeared to be a badly beaten young man in the hospital bed. A magenta color mirroring the evening sky spread across the portion of head peeking out from beneath a swath of bandages and above an oxygen mask. More bandages wrapped the body lying beneath a light blanket. Tubes ran from machines to arms and back to the machines as lit screens indicated the condition of the young man. The stillness and the sterile hospital smell reminded Rex of the morgue, where he seemed to spend way too much time. I really do need to increase my social life and get out more he thought. And then relief flooded Rex as the monitors beeped loudly, indicating signs of life from the body before him.

"I got here as quickly as I could, Chief. What happened? Looks like somebody really banged this guy up," observed Rex, taking note of the many bruises and bandages. "Who's the victim?" he asked, curious why his boss had called him here personally. Usually, a case started with a call from police dispatch. As head of the homicide unit, Detective Rex Begonia shared a long history working with Police Chief Barney Blueblood, but usually bodies weren't breathing when the chief put Rex on a case.

"I need your help. This is a special situation. It's not a homicide case. And I hope it doesn't become one," said the chief, looking back again at the person in the bed. "This young man is my nephew, Scout. He's been in trouble in the past, but he's turned his life around. He's too young to . . ." The chief choked up.

"I'm sorry . . ." started Rex.

Chief Blueblood quickly recovered, stoically continuing, "He was found unconscious outside the Cash Cow Casino. Head injuries left him in a coma and no witnesses have come forward. Because he was found on tribal property, Spokane Tribal Police have jurisdiction, but the sheriff may be interested too. The casino isn't on the reservation. It's one of those situations where everyone's responsible so no one's responsible. I don't want this case to fall through the cracks."

Just then the oxygen monitor let out a shrill sound and a nurse came rushing into the room. He quickly adjusted the amount of oxygen flowing through the tubes and reassured the visitors.

The chief laid a large hand over his heavy heart. He looked anxious. "You okay, Chief?"

"Let's talk about this back at the office. First thing tomorrow."

"I'll be there."

The chief gave him a thankful look and added, "This is personal."

Rex nodded and left the room. He didn't even notice the elderly patient hobbling down the hallway, grasping the pole of a mobile IV in one hand while attempting to hold his hospital gown closed over his bare buttocks with the other. As Rex passed, the old man turned his backside so it was hidden against a decorative paradise palm plant. Nice *Howea forsterance*, thought the detective absently before switching back to problem-solving mode.

Fortunately for Rex, his favorite cafe was just a couple of blocks south of the hospital. Cafe Noir was almost a second home for him. He could sit at his preferred table by the window and slip into thought while tuning out the lively chatter of patrons at surrounding tables and the clanking of plates and cutlery from behind the deli counter. The soft glow from the hanging lights and the colorful cocktails contrasted with the usual roomful of sunshine and coffee drinks that prevailed during the mornings when Rex sat ruminating at what he considered his personal table.

"What brings you in this evening, Rex?" asked raven-haired Gina, his favorite barista, who was working the late shift today so she could take the weekend off. She unobtrusively moved a couple to another table so Rex could sit at "his" table.

"I just came from the hospital," he replied. "Visiting a patient. Thought I'd grab a cup of coffee and do a little thinking." He sank gratefully into his seat and peered out the window into the gathering dusk.

Gina liked Rex and was accustomed to his brevity. He was friendly but not much of a conversationalist. And besides, he always left a generous tip. As she returned to the bar to concoct his standard coffee drink, a Vatican, she shook her head, amazed that he could think with all the hubbub happening in the room. Cafe Noir was packed with couples and small groups of friends and neighbors meeting for dinner and sharing the latest news in their lives.

Rex had no difficulty concentrating amidst all the activity. Having grown up in a large Italian American family in Spokane's Logan neighborhood, he was accustomed to people and noise around him at all times. As an adult, Rex enjoyed the peace and quiet of his solitary home but could still focus inward while surrounded by crowds. And now, the smell of a strong-roasted espresso with Frangelico and a hint of cardamom wafted toward his nose, triggering his analytic brain. He recalled meeting his boss's nephew just once, about eight years ago during a Spokane Police Guild picnic. At the time, Scout must have been about 15-years old. He was quiet and shy. He also had a great throwing arm, helping his uncle's team win the baseball game at the picnic. Rex was curious to learn what the young man had been doing since that day so long ago and what happened recently to land him in a hospital bed.

Chief Barney Blueblood was a well-respected leader of the city's police force. Spokane Mayor Sammy Prosciutto promoted Blueblood to chief three years ago in an effort to reform government in the Lilac City and to deflect accusations of corruption and nepotism. The mayor hated the stereotype of Italian mobsters with their connections to shady politicians. And yet, three of the mayor's siblings worked for the city. Albeit they were on the payroll before he became mayor. Another brother owned a Las Vegas casino where Sammy worked in his younger days. When Sammy Prosciutto promoted the straight arrow Barney Blueblood to the top police position, it improved the mayor's own reputation in the skeptical community. It didn't hurt that Chief Blueblood was a Spokane Indian either. That helped dispel the mobster stereotype. At the end of the day, Rex appreciated that Chief Blueblood was a buffer between the mayor and the police force.

Having finished his coffee, Rex was ready for his next course. For that, he would see what items in the deli caught his fancy. He could take dinner home and enjoy a relaxing evening among his extensive collection of plants and books. As Rex left the cafe with his precious meal of lasagna and a Caesar salad, a young couple absorbed in each other ran into him, nearly knocking his dinner out of his hands. "Hey . . ." began Rex.

"Sorry, old man. Don't take it personal," the young man remarked insolently and rushed right past him.

Personal. There's that word again, thought Rex, remembering his earlier conversation with Chief Blueblood.

Chapter 2

TEAM PLAYER

Wednesday Morning

The next morning, Spokane's top homicide detective arrived at the office early enough to grind his own coffee beans and make a cappuccino prior to meeting with Chief Blueblood. Rex, as usual, chose to skip the communal pot with watered down coffee and use his own espresso machine and beans. As a result, his colleagues considered him a coffee snob. Ostensibly, Rex argued that a decent cup of coffee was necessary for the brain to tackle complicated criminal cases.

One of those colleagues, Sergeant Phil O'Dendren entered the office break room. Next to Rex's partner Ivy and the chief, the sergeant was probably the nearest the detective had to a close friend in the department. Rex and the burly, ginger-haired cop were colleagues for almost 20 years. Despite their many differences, both men worked hard and took pride in serving on the Spokane police force. O'Dendren was friendly and outgoing. And, unlike Rex, he enjoyed interacting with the public.

"Hey Rex, how'd you like to help make the Spokane Police Department famous?" O'Dendren asked as he poured a cup of coffee from the communal pot and picked up a bear claw pastry from a plate of mostly crumbs.

"Famous? Famous for what?" asked Rex, wondering what scheme O'Dendren had planned.

"This is the year the Spokane Police Department wins the Bloomsday Corporate Cup. At least it was until Officer Silva tore a ligament in his knee during a drug bust. It looks like he might not be ready to run in Bloomsday in three weeks. He was our ace runner. So, we need someone to take his place on the department's corporate cup team."

"The fire department has some new recruits. Used to run for EWU. They're boasting they'll take the cup this year. We want to show them what the boys and girls in blue can do," explained the sergeant.

The Lilac Bloomsday Run was a 7.46 mile race through the heart of the city. Every first Sunday in May for four decades, about 50,000 runners, walkers and wheelchair athletes proved their fitness, or not, in one of the largest, timed, road races in the world. Racers traveled from countries around the world to participate and vie for the prize money and fame. The Spokane firefighters' team, The Heat, won the corporate cup for the past five years.

All of Spokane turned out for the race, whether as participants, volunteers, or viewers along the race route. Rex ran every Bloomsday for twenty years and always placed in the top 150 racers. Now that he was in his fifth decade, he opted to volunteer. Besides, he owned more Bloomsday t-shirts than he knew what to do with.

Rex's first inclination was to decline. He didn't want to be part of a team. "I haven't run regularly for the past four years. I would need to get in better shape," he rationalized. Then he thought about carbo-loading on pasta. Hmmm. Incentive enough. "When do you need an answer? I'm supposed to be meeting with the chief," he said, looking at his watch.

"Don't think about it too long. We've got practice tomorrow at 5:00 a.m. Meet here at the office. We run along the Centennial Trail and loop through the park," said O'Dendren.

Rex nodded to his colleague and sprinted down the hall to the chief's office.

"Getting ready for Bloomsday?" the chief asked Rex, who caught his breath as he sat down across the desk from Barney Blueblood. At six-feet, four-inches and with broad shoulders, Chief Blueblood cut an imposing figure. His short, dark hair, graying at the temples, framed a serious face that belied his sense of humor. Even under cross-examination, the chief was known to have a dry wit.

Rex attempted a smile. "Sorry to get here late, Chief. How's your nephew? Any improvement?"

"He's stable. Thanks for asking," replied Chief Blueblood. "He took quite a beating. It looked like whoever did it left him for dead. He was lucky though. He couldn't have been there for long before a couple of casino kitchen hands out for a smoke found him behind a dumpster and called for help."

A curious case of smoking saving a life, thought Rex. Wait until the tobacco lobby hears of this. "The Cash Cow Casino? Isn't that out of our jurisdiction, Chief?" he asked. "That's in Airway Heights. Doesn't that fall under the county's jurisdiction? Or would the tribal police be handling the case because the casino is tribal property and the victim is a Spokane Indian? Jurisdictional issues can be tricky."

"You're right. It is tricky," said Blueblood. "But, my younger brother Andy is the Spokane Tribal Police Chief. Yeah, it runs in the family. He's also Scout's father. In this case, I think I can convince Andy to request assistance from the Spokane Police Department and I'll have a talk with Sheriff Annie Wyatt to make sure we're cooperating with the county. Don't start the investigation until I've had a chance to clear it with the tribe and the county. Remember, this is personal.

"When Scout was in high school, he started hanging out with a bad crowd. He began doing drugs, then selling drugs. Scout and Andy had a falling out. It was quite the scandal when the tribal police chief's son was implicated in drug dealing. Scout spent a couple of years in juvenile detention and when he was released, I brought him home with me. Put him in rehab. He cleaned up, earned his GED and got a job at Tom's Taxidermy Shop in the Hillyard area of town." While he spoke, Chief Blueblood haphazardly shuffled items around his desk.

"We bonded during his early years when his dad and I took him hunting. Scout felt comfortable with me and I've been mentoring him the past ten years. He was doing well. He even started talking about going to college and studying anthropology. But recently, one of his old buddies showed up. Scout started staying out late and avoided inquiries about where he was and who he was with. I suspect the beating had something to do with his old friend and whatever they were involved with.

"This has to be hard for my brother," Blueblood sighed heavily and rubbed his eyes. "Despite their falling out, he loves Scout as deeply as any father loves a son. They had just started getting back on track before this happened. My brother's a professional and as the Spokane Tribal Police Chief, he'll make every effort to investigate thoroughly, no matter where it leads him. But as a father, I'm sure he'll accept any help we offer. I know you don't like multi-jurisdictional work, but you're our best detective Rex. I'm asking you as a friend, not your boss, to help on this case."

It was true, Rex Begonia was Spokane's top detective. Homicide detective that is. And this wasn't a murder case. He much preferred to investigate alone without the complications of working with other people and especially with other departments. A few years ago, Chief Blueblood pointedly directed him to interact more within his own department and even assigned Rex to mentor the young and diminutive Junior Detective Ivy Lizei as his partner. Ivy had surprised Rex with her excellent investigative skills and physical strength while helping solve the Murder at Manito Case and bringing the perpetrator to justice last year.

"How about Ivy? Is she assigned to this case too, Chief?" Rex asked.

"Good idea. She could use the multi-jurisdictional experience. In fact, there's a multi-agency training taking place in Seattle later this month. It's being headed up by the FBI. See if there are any openings. If there are, I'd like you to both register to attend."

Now what have I done, thought Rex. He hadn't intended to get involved with the Federal Bureau of Investigation. Switching back to the case at hand, he asked, "When can I speak with Scout?"

"That's the problem. He's in a coma. The doctors don't know how long it will be until we can talk with him," answered the chief. "We've got no witnesses and a contaminated crime scene. It's more complicated than investigating a homicide with a body of evidence."

Chapter 3

LAYING THE GROUNDWORK

Wednesday Afternoon

Rex was browsing through a cold case file and eating a salami sandwich for lunch at his desk when Ivy Lizei bounded into the office. She had spent the morning at the Spokane County Forensics Unit, which processed much of the city's crime scene evidence. Her thick, red hair pulled back in a ponytail, flounced as she fixed her almond-shaped green eyes on the senior detective and smiled.

"Hi Boss, what's new?" she asked in her bubbly manner.

"The chief wants us to attend a law enforcement interagency training in Seattle next month," replied Rex. "And he has a new case for us, but I can't tell you much about it until he's laid some groundwork."

"Well, now that just makes me curious. Are the case and the training related?" asked Ivy as she hung her Kelly-green trench coat on a hook behind her desk. To find the hook hiding among a veritable jungle surrounding her desk, she had to move fronds of an asparagus fern hanging off the shelves.

Rex appreciated Ivy's love of plants. The plant population in the office more than tripled when she joined the force. And that spoke volumes because he owned his own extensive plant collection in the office. The office was beginning to take on the appearance of a botanical garden. *We're doing our part to clean the air in here*, thought Rex, as he watched Ivy search for the hook.

"This case will require inter-agency cooperation but the chief thought it would be good for us to attend the training either way. There are a couple of slots still open. Can you clear your schedule for the last week of April?"

Ivy looked at the calendar on her phone. Technology was second nature to her, unlike for her old-school mentor who still kept a large calendar on his wall next to a map of the city. "I can skip my Aikido class that week and reschedule my 2:30 dentist appointment for another day," mused Ivy. "That's the week before Bloomsday. I'll have to take my running gear with me if I want to stay in shape. I don't want to let down the rest of the team."

"Are you on the department's corporate cup team?" asked Rex, not sure he wanted to showcase his lack of fitness to his partner.

"Sure am, Boss," Ivy answered proudly. She had overcome her colleagues' hesitancy to her presence after joining the male-dominated force. Not only was she female, but she only stood four-feet, ten-inches. The men had doubted her physical abilities as a cop. Ivy earned their respect after using a ninja move on a co-worker who had pulled a prank on her shortly after she joined the force. "Sergeant O'Dendren said he thinks we can win the corporate cup this year. That was before Silva got injured though. Hopefully, O'Dendren can find a replacement that's just as fast."

Rex's brow furrowed. "Well bring your running gear to Seattle. I'll try to keep up with you," he said.

"Oh, Boss, that's great! Does that mean you're joining the department's corporate cup team? Sergeant O'Dendren said he was going to ask you. There're some killer hills in Seattle. We can really get in shape for the race!"

"Yeah, I'll let O'Dendren know that I'll run," said Rex, wondering once again what he might be getting into. He could visualize the headline – Seattle Killer Hill Finishes Off Spokane Homicide Cop.

"Great! Thanks! So, what about the new case? What can you tell me?" Ivy asked.

"A young man was found badly beaten outside the Cash Cow Casino yesterday. He's in a coma in the hospital. Chief Blueblood would like us to find out who did it. The young man is the chief's nephew." He let Ivy process that last bit of information. "The investigation will involve working with the tribal police and possibly the sheriff's office. The chief has to lay some groundwork with the other agencies before we get started."

"Cool. Sounds intriguing. It'll be real interagency work, not just training." Although Ivy's academic credentials were exemplary, she much preferred on-the-job training over classroom instruction.

"Speaking of training, I've been meaning to talk with you. The Washington Department of Fish and Wildlife has asked if I would help with a self-defense training the department is putting on for new recruits. They're trying to hire more women enforcement officers. Beau Hunter figured with me being a female and with my martial arts skills, I could help inspire the female recruits. What do you think, Boss, could the Spokane Police Department spare me for a day?"

More like recruit Ivy, worried Rex. "Who's Beau Hunter and when is the training?" he asked. Then added, "We'll have to run it by the chief."

"It's not for awhile yet. Late May. Beau just wanted to get the date on my calendar. Beau Hunter's a wildlife officer I met about a month ago. He works in the Fish and Wildlife Department's Investigative and Enforcement Unit. Anyway, we've sort of been seeing each other since then. We ate lunch at that new Korean restaurant Tofucious on the north side of town today and he mentioned the training."

"Well, we could probably spare you for a day. As long as the wildlife folks don't start poaching the Spokane Police Department's talent," grumbled Rex. "We'll get Chief Blueblood's blessing when we talk with him later about the case with his nephew." He looked back at the cold case file on his desk. So, Ivy was dating a wildlife officer? He would have to meet the guy. Rex, who was single and didn't have children of his own, felt a fatherly protection toward his mentee.

Ivy hoped Rex would ask her about Beau. She wanted to share her excitement about her new boyfriend and besides, she valued her mentor's opinion. He was a good judge of character.

Fifteen minutes of quiet passed with only the sound of Ivy tapping on her keyboard. Not ready to abandon the conversation, she looked up from her computer and asked, "Have you heard rumors about devil worshippers in Rathdrum?"

That got Rex's attention. What did devil worshippers have to do with anything? He gave Ivy a perplexed expression. "Devil worshippers?"

"Yeah. Beau told me about an interesting case he's working on. Some mushroom hunters found a horse carcass in the woods north of Newman

Lake. It was tied to a tree and was all black, like it had been burned. The mushroom hunters reported it to the sheriff's office. They thought devil worshippers used the horse as a sacrifice in some satanic ritual. They claimed there've been devil worshippers in North Idaho for the past 30 years. Even though the horse was found in Washington, it was only about 20 miles from Rathdrum."

"That is odd," remarked Rex, frowning.

"When Beau and the other wildlife officers investigated the horse and the site, they determined it was a case of illegal bear baiting," continued Ivy. "Apparently, hunters have been known to attract black bears using dead livestock. In this case, the decomposition was such that it looked like someone intentionally set fire to the body. According to Beau, illegal bear baiting is on the increase."

"Seems like a dead, burned horse could scare mushroom hunters from trespassing on your favorite mushroom foraging area too," commented Rex. After all, mushroom foragers could rival Los Angeles gangs when it came to protecting their fungi turf. But then again, strange stories grew out of the forests of North Idaho and Northeast Washington.

Chief Blueblood approached carrying a folder which he laid on Rex's desk. "I've arranged for you two to meet with Tribal Police Chief Andy Blueblood tomorrow at 9:00 a.m. at the Cash Cow Casino. Check in at the front desk. He'll fill you in on what the Tribal Police know about Scout's assault. I'm assuming you've told Ivy about this assignment, Rex?"

Rex nodded.

"Andy will arrange for you to talk with Louie, the casino manager, and the two kitchen workers who found Scout. Also, Sheriff Wyatt confirmed that unless any information turns up to indicate this incident extends beyond the casino property or that non-Indians were involved, this is the Spokane Tribe's jurisdiction. Just keep Wyatt apprised if you learn anything that would indicate the county should get involved."

"Thanks Chief. How's your nephew doing?" Rex asked.

"Still in a coma, but at least he's stable. I appreciate you both setting aside the time to work on this case."

"No worries, Chief. It's been a bit quiet in the murder business lately," deadpanned Rex.

"Thanks for letting me work on the case, too," Ivy added, suppressing a laugh. "And since things are slow, would you also approve me assisting the Department of Fish and Wildlife with self-defense training?"

"Well, you two are really getting into the spirit of multi-agency work. Have the department put the request in a letter and I'll approve it," Chief Blueblood answered happily. "Always good to help another agency. You never know when we might need the favor returned." He went back to his office while Rex and Ivy resumed their respective tasks, forgetting about Beau, horse carcasses and devil worshippers for the rest of the afternoon.

As he left the office later, Rex had forgotten about his Bloomsday promise too. But Sergeant Phil O'Dendren and Ivy met him at the door.

"Don't forget – 5 a.m. run tomorrow," they called in unison.

Rex groaned.

Chapter 4

OFF AND RUNNING

Thursday Morning

It was still dark at 4:53 a.m. when Rex showed up at the designated meeting spot, the clock tower in Riverfront Park. And it was raining. Garbage trucks rattled through the empty city streets picking up trash before cars and busses filled with commuters descended upon downtown. He shivered in the chill, moist air – anxious to warm up by running. Ivy had already arrived and was stretching her legs against the brick wall of the tower.

"Morning, Boss!"

How could she sound so perky?! Rex hadn't even drunk his coffee yet. He mumbled a reply as he jogged in place to warm up.

Before the clock struck five, Sergeant Phil O'Dendren and officers Scott Pine, known on the force as Hollywood, and Bruce Hemlock joined them. They all wore headlamps and yellow reflective vests over their cool-weather running clothes. "Let's get moving before we freeze like statues," suggested O'Dendren, his breath visible in the light of his headlamp.

They ran north and east along the Centennial Trail as it followed the path of the winding river out of the park, past the Gonzaga University campus and along the edge of the Logan neighborhood where Rex grew up. He was thankful for the primarily flat path while he huffed and puffed to keep up with the others. The trail smelled of earthworms crawling from the saturated soil to commit suicide on the path. He would have to investigate closer some rainy day. As the group neared their turning around point, the clouds parted and the sun rose, creating a soft golden glow. The top of Mount Spokane, white with fresh snow, rose above the valley. At least for the moment, Rex was thankful for having woken early.

"Not bad," said O'Dendren as he checked his watch after arriving back at the clock tower. "Next week, we'll choose a route with a hill. We need to get ready for that long, steep stretch up Doomsday Hill."

Rex was beginning to view the whole experience as Doomsday as he panted to catch his breath. He had certainly warmed up! Fortunately, he could shower and change at the office before starting work.

After cleaning up, the senior detective attended the daily staff briefing and drank his second cappuccino of the morning. He felt ready to start on the Scout Blueblood case. He went outside where Ivy pulled up in an unmarked, black Crown Vic at the front of the building to pick him up.

"Have you ever wondered about the phrase riding shotgun?" Ivy asked, as Rex climbed into the passenger seat. She didn't even wait for him to answer. "It originated in the Old West. Stagecoach drivers had shotgun-toting partners next to them for protection. So, you're my gun-toting partner."

Sometimes Ivy's predilection for chit-chat amazed Rex, who was quite introverted. It was one of her many characteristics that first annoyed him when they were assigned to work together, but that he eventually came to appreciate. As they drove the half hour to the casino, he reviewed with her the complexities of law enforcement jurisdiction they faced on this case. Unless officers regularly worked with Indian tribes, they could overlook what they learned about tribal jurisdiction long ago in basic training.

When they arrived, the partners made their way through what seemed like acres of cars in the parking lot. Bunchgrass plants lined a flagstone walkway, skirting the small pond beside the casino. Water cascaded down from a basalt column fountain at one end of the pond. A gentle breeze whispered through the grass plants as the fountain burbled softly. The transition made for a jarring juxtaposition as Rex and Ivy walked through the tall, glass doors into the noisy, bustling casino.

Inside the building, slot machines clanged and patrons shouted out numbers at the gaming tables. The two detectives wove through the smoke-filled room of players sitting intently before the slot machines. Rex gave Indians credit for seven-generation thinking. They were slowly taking wealth back from the white man. And it was being done voluntarily! As they approached the other side of the main gaming room, a man who could be Chief Barney Blueblood's slightly shorter double stepped forward to meet them.

"Welcome to the Cash Cow Casino," said Police Chief Andy Blueblood, extending a hand in greeting. "You must be detectives Begonia and Lizei. Thank you for coming."

"How did you know it was us?" Ivy asked incredulously.

"Most people come here looking like they want a good time," answered the tribal police chief. "No offense, but you look like cops on the clock. Easy targets for con artists," he added with a twinkle in his eyes, while leading them into a small meeting room. "All kidding aside, the casino has been an economic boon for our tribe. We've been able to hire hundreds of our tribal members and give them decent wages. We've also invested a large share of the profits into educating our youth and providing essential services for our elders."

"Impressive," remarked Rex, looking around the room. Large, Native American paintings decorated the walls and a plush carpet with an Indian motif covered the floor. Pendleton throws were draped over the lodge-style sofas in the corner. The group sat down at a table made of Lodgepole pine timbers. The decor showed off the economic gains the Spokanes made in recent years while still keeping true to their distinctive indigenous style.

"Would you like some coffee?" asked Andy as a waiter from the casino restaurant brought in a tray containing coffee, tea and huckleberry scones.

How could Rex resist?

"Tea please," said Ivy.

After the waiter poured beverages and left the room, Andy said, "I want to thank you for offering to help find Scout's attacker. You know that I'm Chief Barney Blueblood's younger brother and the police chief for the Spokane Tribe. Our father, grandfather and great-grandfather were warriors, fighting first for our tribe and then for the United States in America's wars. Our mother's ancestors were chiefs of the Coeur d' Alenes. We've served our communities for generations."

Nodding toward the detectives, Andy added, "My brother speaks highly of you both and praised your investigative skills."

"Thank you," said Rex. "We're fortunate to have your brother as our police chief. He's well-respected in the community and I've had the pleasure of working with him for many years. Ivy's still fairly new on the force but I think you will find your brother's assessment of her skills accurate."

Ivy blushed with pride.

"That's good because we don't have much information to go on. And this is a sensitive situation with the victim being my son," admitted the tribal police chief. "Let me give you some background and then we'll call in the employees that found him unconscious behind the casino.

"Scout got in trouble a few years back when he was in high school. Got involved with drugs, even selling them. He did some time in juvenile detention. He cleaned up and was getting his life back on track, thanks in large part to my brother. But then Scout's best friend from high school, Danny Darkfoot, showed up last fall. Danny had been in prison.

"I think Scout got tangled up in some criminal activity with Danny and whoever else he might have been involved with these last few months. I tried to discourage him from associating with Danny, but it didn't do any good. He always learned things the hard way instead of listening to his elders.

"When Scout was found beaten up, I went looking for Danny hoping he could tell me what happened. Not that he'd want to talk with me," Andy admitted before continuing, "I haven't found him yet. He was living in an old house on the reservation. My officers have been watching for him, but he hasn't turned up. If he doesn't show up soon, we'll put up missing person posters on the reservation and here at the casino. He easily could be lying low in Spokane or anywhere around here."

"Is there anyone in the community Danny was close with? Someone we could talk to?" asked Ivy.

"He was close with his grandmother. I checked with her and she hasn't seen him either. But, I'll give you her contact information in case you want to get in touch with her."

"How about any other theories? Would there be anyone else that might have a reason for assaulting Scout? Or, could it have been an attempted robbery? Could he have just won a pile of money at the casino and been followed out by someone who took the winnings?" Rex asked.

"Let's get the manager, Louie, in here before we go much further," said Andy. He called the manager's office on his phone and then turned back to the two detectives. "Nothing seemed to be missing when Scout arrived at the hospital. He still had his wallet. And his bear claw pendant and a silver bracelet that he wears were still on him."

Louie arrived. Chief Andy Blueblood introduced him to the Spokane detectives, explaining they were helping with the Scout Blueblood case. The two detectives rose, shook hands with the casino manager and offered him their business cards.

"What can you tell us about the incident earlier this week?" Rex asked the manager after resuming his seat.

"One of the cooks and a dishwasher discovered him. They were on their afternoon break. Joe, the dishwasher, came running into the kitchen area yelling for someone to call 9-1-1 and that there was a guy bleeding by the dumpster. One of the waitresses called while a couple of the floor workers and I ran outside. Most of the staff have extensive first aid training. Lot of fainting and heart attacks with jackpot winners," explained the manager.

"We found him on the ground with blood everywhere. It looked like someone hit him a bunch of times in the face. Must've fallen hitting his head against the dumpster. He was still breathing though. And he had a pulse. We figured he couldn't have been there very long. A few minutes I'd guess. The EMTs got there real fast. They took over but they never did get him conscious before taking him to the hospital."

"How about police? When did police arrive?" Rex asked.

"Officer Schlotts was the first to respond. He arrived before the EMTs left. Once he recognized Scout, he contacted me directly," said Andy. "I turned on the lights and drove here in about 35 minutes. Officer Schlotts questioned the kitchen workers and after I arrived, we swept the immediate area looking for clues or anything that might have been dropped in the struggle. After searching the area, we reviewed the casino's security camera footage with Louie."

"He didn't show up on any of the interior cameras, or any out in front of the casino," added Louie. "One of the cameras in back caught a glimpse of him at 2:48 p.m. He was with someone else, but I couldn't see the face. Whoever it was wore a hoodie."

"No one on the gambling floor saw Scout that afternoon. I checked," continued Andy. "He didn't appear to be gambling. So that shoots the theory about stealing gambling winnings."

Louie brought up the video footage on his computer screen and enlarged the picture. In it, a young Indian man dressed in jeans and a faded red t-shirt walked in and out of view. A long, black braid hung down his back. His head was turned toward another person who walked beside and slightly behind him. The person wore dark clothing. The person's size and broad shoulders indicated a man. A sweatshirt hood covered the portion of his head visible behind Scout.

The casino manager excused himself and returned with the first of the two kitchen workers, who verified the manager's story. The second kitchen worker told the same account, adding only that he knew Scout Blueblood and saw him meeting people at the casino in the past. The only person he recognized with Scout on those occasions was Danny Darkfoot. The others were white males, but he didn't know any of them.

"What about drugs?" asked Ivy. "Was it a possible drug deal that went bad?"

Andy winced. "I'd like to say we could rule that out, but I don't think we can," he admitted. "Which brings us back to Danny. If Scout got involved with drugs again, Danny would know."

"Until Scout comes out of his coma, it looks like this case starts with tracking Danny Darkfoot then," observed Rex. "Since we're already about a quarter of the way to the Spokane Reservation, let's see if we can meet with Danny Darkfoot's grandmother this afternoon and save some driving."

The younger Chief Blueblood called ahead to arrange the appointment. Danny's grandmother, Winnie Milne, agreed to a visit if the two detectives could be at her house in 45 minutes. They would have to leave right away, skipping lunch.

Between the morning run and missed lunch, Rex was hungry. He could hear his stomach growling.

Chapter 5

TRACKING DANNY DARKFOOT

Thursday Afternoon

When Rex and Ivy arrived at the small, one-story, gray house on the edge of the reservation, they were met by snarling, black hounds. An elderly woman in a pale, yellow dress decorated with blue flowers opened the door and called the dogs inside. She put the dogs in a back room and then returned to invite the detectives indoors. Rex detected the fragrant smell of muffins baking, which only peaked his appetite.

"I'm Winifred Milne," she said, "You can call me Winnie. Sorry about the dogs. They belong to Danny. They've been ill-tempered since Danny disappeared," she explained. She led the detectives into a cozy living room and to Rex's delight offered them coffee. He hoped the coffee came with muffins.

"Do you have any tea?" asked Ivy, politely.

They waited on an overstuffed green couch with a multi-colored afghan throw on the back and looked up at a shelf covered with family photographs, pine baskets, a pair of beaded baby moccasins and a *Tolmiea* plant. "We're here to learn what you can tell us about Danny," said Rex, as Mrs. Milne set down a tray with two mugs of black coffee, a cup of tea and a basket of warm muffins and honey. Rex smiled.

The elderly woman sat down near them on a matching green chair. Wispy, white hair framed her pinched, wrinkled face and was pulled back with a beaded hair clip. She looked sad. "Danny is the youngest son of my second daughter Annie," she started. "They lived in Montana until his father died when Danny was eleven. That's when they moved back here to the reservation."

She told them how Danny's mom struggled with alcohol and unemployment after returning home and how it affected the boy. He had difficulty with school and making friends. By the time he was in high school, Danny was mixed up with drugs. He was arrested and put in juvenile detention. He couldn't stay out of trouble and ended up in prison as an adult. After his release nine months ago, he moved back to the reservation again to live with Winnie.

"He was cursed with his father's blood," complained Danny's grandmother. "If only Annie had stayed here and married her own kind, her son would have grown up proper. But he possessed his mother's blood too, so he wasn't all bad. Danny was good to me and helped with chores around here.

"Now I am worried about him. I fear something bad may have happened to him. A week before he disappeared, I had a dream." Winnie took a sip of coffee and then elaborated. "In the dream, a group of young men played the spear-ring game. Danny was one of the young men. They played in a clearing in the forest. Two short walls made from saplings stood at either end of the clearing. A large, white man with a bushy brown beard rolled a ring into the clearing toward one of the walls. The ring was made from willow branches wrapped together with strips of willow bark. The men shot arrows at the ring. Old men sat around the clearing betting on the young men and exchanging money."

Winnie continued, "A gust of wind swooped through the clearing. It picked up one of Danny's arrows and blew it toward the bearded man. The arrow pierced the man's foot and he cried out in pain. As he screamed, he grew bigger and darker. He transformed into a large brown bear. The men ran but the bear caught Danny and tore him apart.

"I woke up shaking. The spirits were telling me that Danny was in danger," finished Winnie, sadly. Her head dropped and she wrung her small, bony hands together in her lap.

Ivy reached out and placed her hand on Winnie's thin arm. The atmosphere stilled as the conversation fell silent. In the back room, snuffling sounds from the dogs could be heard as they fidgeted behind the closed door.

Finally, Rex asked, "When and where was the last time you saw Danny?"

"He was here at the house," Winnie answered. "It was two days ago. He brought me groceries and helped with chores around here. Carried in some fire wood, stuff like that. Then he told me he would be gone hunting for awhile and left the dogs with me. That was odd. He usually takes the dogs hunting.

"Since being back on the reservation, he's earned money hunting. He and a friend do some work for a hunting guide in Spokane. Danny's a good boy. He's filled my freezer with meat, and he's given meat to other elders."

"Is his hunting friend Scout Blueblood?" questioned Ivy.

"Yes. They've hunted together since they were young boys. Scout's father and uncle took them hunting and taught them the ways of our people. I heard about what happened to Scout. I am worried Danny may be hurt too," Winnie added.

"We'll find him," Rex reassured her. "What was he driving when he left?"

"He has an old gray van. I don't know the license number. I think it's a Chevy. It has a stripe and a window on the side."

"Can you tell us the name of the hunting guide? And anyone else you can think of that might know where Danny would have gone?"

"Just a minute," said Winnie, as she rose and then went into a back room.

While she was out of the room, Rex absentmindedly ate a third muffin with honey.

When Winnie returned, she held a camo-colored ball cap in her hand. "This might be the guide," said Winnie, pointing to the Varmint Outfitters' name and logo on the cap. "Danny doesn't tell me much about his hunting and he doesn't write anything down. Any phone numbers or information are in his phone."

A downside to technology, thought Rex. Fewer physical tracks. But maybe they could at least get a photograph. He stood up and perused the family photos on the shelf. "Is there a recent picture of Danny that you could let us borrow? It would help to know what he looks like if we hope to find him."

Winnie chose a photo of Danny playing with the dogs and handed it to the detective. "This was taken a year ago. It's the last picture I have of him." She sounded blue.

Rex looked closely at the picture. The young Indian wore his black hair short with bangs. The detective was surprised to see that Danny was smaller than average but appeared wiry and strong. He bore a tattoo with text on the right side of his neck. Winnie explained that it was a Salish word for family. Tattoos of mountains and a coyote decorated his bared arms.

"Thank you," said Rex, while accepting the picture. "I hope to bring this back along with Danny." Silently, he fervently hoped Danny would be alive when they returned.

Chapter 6

THE BET

Thursday Evening

After arriving back at the precinct and finishing out the day, Rex drove to his parents' house for the weekly Begonia family dinner. Ivy had opted to join a few of their colleagues at the 24-hour Hole-in-One Donut Shop for some after work socializing. Not exactly Rex's cup of tea. But then he preferred coffee anyway.

Dinner at the Begonia house in the Logan neighborhood was the highlight of the week for Rex. As he walked in the door, the savory smell of Bolognese sauce simmering for hours on the stove emanated from the kitchen, filling the home with a welcoming fragrance. Mama Begonia, bedecked in her red checked apron, lifted a pot lid and slid spaghetti noodles into the boiling, salted water. Rex leaned over and kissed her nearest rosy cheek. "Delizioso!" exclaimed Rex.

"Me or the spaghetti?" laughed Mama, giving the sauce a stir.

"What's new, Rex?" asked Sophia as she handed him a bowl of salad to put on the table. Sophia, the youngest of his five siblings, was married to Chef Nobu Hiyamugi, who was the only other person who could rival Mama Begonia at making spaghetti Bolognese.

"Somehow, I've found myself on a Bloomsday corporate cup team at work. I only have two weeks to get in shape for the race," bemoaned Rex. "I might need to come over three or four times a week to carbo-load on pasta."

"You do that and we'll be rolling you along the race route," teased his older sister Martina, who took the salad bowl from him and delivered it to the dining room table.

The rest of the Begonia family began to wander into the kitchen like vultures to a fresh kill. Older brother Nick pinched a breadstick while Rex snuck a bit of anchovy paste to Tonno the striped cat, who had sidled up to his leg.

"Out! Out! Go wash up." Mama Begonia good-naturedly shooed everyone out of the kitchen so she could drain the noodles, remove the sauce from the stove and get the dinner on the table while it was still hot.

As usual, the dinner was a cacophony of conversations as parents, siblings, spouses, nieces and nephews exchanged news about the week's events. It was vastly different from his own quiet house, yet Rex felt completely at home.

"How's the restaurant doing?" Nick asked brother-in-law Nobu. "I heard that the Korean Market opened an adjoining restaurant, Tofucious, and it's killing the competition."

Nobu, seated next to his wife Sophia, the youngest Begonia, answered, "Ha, if I worried about competition, I never would have opened an Asian restaurant in Spokane."

Rex had to agree. Asian restaurants in Spokane were as numerous as coffee shops in Seattle.

The conversation turned toward the upcoming race. At least seven other family members planned to run or walk Bloomsday. Everyone guessed what color the Bloomsday finisher t-shirt would be this year. Most Begonias bet on green. The color and design were always a well-kept secret until the first finishers concluded the race. Mama announced she planned to cook a big pasta dinner the evening before the race. Fortunately, she made her own noodles because it was one time of the year that Spokane grocery stores couldn't keep enough pasta on the shelves!

On the other side of town, another Bloomsday wager was unfolding. Ivy and her fellow police officers encountered a group of Spokane firefighters at the Hole-in-One Donut Shop. The firefighters from Station One also had formed a corporate cup team – The Heat – and registered for the big race.

"You cream puffs don't stand a chance against my boys. We've won every year for the last five years," Chief Billy Blaize boomed in his loud voice after learning the police entered a corporate cup team in the race this year. The tall man with red hair and matching walrus-style mustache marched up to the table where Ivy and the others were seated. "Come on O'Dendren.

Let's put some money on the race. You Irish will bet on anything, even if it is a losing cause."

Ivy glanced over at the table of firefighters. They looked like they hauled 200-pound bodies out of burning buildings every day. And they weren't all boys either. Two of the firefighters were women and they, too, looked like they could be on an Olympic weightlifting team. But could they run? Ivy, who at four-feet, ten-inches could throw someone more than twice her weight with a ninja move, knew that looks could be deceiving. Martial arts skills didn't make up for her short legs, though, and Ivy worried she might be the weak link on her team.

"I'm not in the habit of losing," O'Dendren shot back. "This year, the winning team will be wearing blue. You fireflies think you're so hot. We'll cool your flames. I'll bet you a hundred bucks our Flatfoots douse your Heat."

"You're on." Chief Blaize's expression lit up with anticipation.

"Let's make it a little more interesting. If you beat us, we'll wash your team's fire trucks. If we win, your officers wash our team's police vehicles," said Chief Blueblood, who had joined his officers at the donut shop and couldn't resist a friendly wager with his pal Fire Chief Billy Blaize.

"Yeah!" shouted officers Pine and Silva, waving their fists toward the firefighters. The rivalry heated the room quickly.

Oh no, thought Ivy. They would have to win now. What would Rex think of this?

Chapter 7

A FOWL BUSINESS

Friday Morning

Rex was sore. O'Dendren started their workout at 4:30 a.m. The team had run the race route plus three extra miles! What had gotten into him to join O'Dendren's madness? There was barely time to clean up if Rex wanted to stop for a quick cappuccino at Cafe Noir before going into the office.

"Hey, Boss, I've found contact info for Varmint Outfitters," said Ivy, looking up from her computer as Rex entered the room with a cup of espresso. She smiled knowing it wasn't his first cup. "Says here that the owner is Boone Crockett and he has an office on the north side of town. According to his website, he specializes in guiding big game hunts in Eastern Washington and North Idaho. Wow! There's some big money in this business. Look at the prices! Hiring these guides would cost me a month's wages!"

"Good job. How about an address?" Rex asked.

After hearing the address, he remarked, "That's in the Hillyard neighborhood. Chief Blueblood mentioned that Scout works at Tom's Taxidermy on the north end of town. Let's find out if Boone Crockett or Tom, the taxidermist, can shed any light on what happened to Danny and Scout. We don't have any other leads and we don't even know if Danny's disappearance has anything to do with the attack on Scout. Chief Blueblood and his brother seemed to think so, though."

"If we're in Hillyard, maybe we can stop at that new Korean restaurant, Tofucious," recommended Ivy.

"Now you're talking." Rex wasn't going to miss lunch two days in a row.

Before heading out of the office, the two detectives checked the background of their interview subjects by doing a bit of online research and preparing dossiers. Rex also took a quick peek at the online restaurant reviews.

"This is interesting," he said aloud. He had run across a *Spokane Lede* news article about a hunter killed while bear hunting with Varmint Outfitters last October. All the guides on the expedition swore it was an accidental shooting. A jury acquitted Varmint Outfitters in the case after determining the death an accident. "I wonder how often that happens on a guided trip?" he asked rhetorically, after reading the full article to Ivy.

"Couldn't be good for business, I would think," she remarked.

By mid-morning, the two detectives were on their way to the Hillyard neighborhood. The Crown Victoria jolted over a series of potholes, rattling Rex's brain and causing Ivy, who was driving, to apologize. "Sorry, Boss. They're unavoidable."

"Yeah, we'll have to send a report to Mayor Prosciutto. He's been negligent lately. He won't get re-elected with these roads."

"Maybe when the chief submits his budget, he could request all four-wheel drives for the police fleet," suggested Ivy. "That would get the mayor's attention."

Ivy parked on Market Street, halfway between the taxidermy shop and the headquarters for Varmint Outfitters. Then they split up with Rex heading toward the guide shop while Ivy ventured in the opposite direction.

The shutters were drawn on the small, dilapidated brick taxidermy shop. White and black letters spelled "Tom's Taxidermy" in peeling paint on a sign above the door. In the window, a red neon "Open" sign blinked, indicating the place was still in business.

Ivy entered the shop. Although a bell on the door chimed to let the shopkeeper know a customer had entered, no one appeared. The room smelled musty. It was dimly lit. As Ivy's eyes adjusted, she saw the heads of elk, deer and moose staring back at her vacantly from the walls. A bighorn sheep fixed its glassy gaze at her from its perch on a boulder floor display. Creepy. She didn't see one plant in the whole store!

A buzzing overhead came from a fly struggling to free itself from a strip of sticky bait. It gave up and joined the other accumulated insect carcasses lining the parchment. Ivy turned toward a dusty counter cluttered with ancient magazines in messy piles and a variety of mounted game birds. She stepped over to the counter and peered more closely at one of the birds.

Just then, a butterball-shaped proprietor with greased-back dark hair waddled out from a back room and approached her.

"That's a fine-looking specimen of a stuffed bird," Ivy said, trying to sound pleasant. "What is it?"

"A sage grouse," replied the shopkeeper. "A little seasoning and they make mighty fine eating."

Ivy thought back to a conversation with Beau. She remembered that even if the sage grouse wasn't protected in Idaho, at least here in Washington, it enjoyed endangered species' protection. What kind of a fowl business was this Tom fellow running?

"You're Tom, I presume?"

"Tom Cathartes. What can I do you for, little lady?"

Due to her diminutive height, Ivy was more than a teeny bit irked at being called a little lady. She took a deep breath to keep from lashing out with a ninja move on this turkey.

"I'm Ivy Lizei, a detective with the Spokane Police Department. I'd like to ask you a few questions about your employee – Scout Blueblood." She showed Tom her badge.

Tom didn't seem so cocky now. He appeared nervous. "What's he done? I haven't seen Scout for a few days."

"I don't know that Scout's done anything wrong. He's in a coma in the hospital. He was found beaten up and unconscious. I was hoping you could tell me what kind of an employee he was. Is there anything he said or did that would cause someone to assault him? Is there anyone he hung out with that might be cause for concern?"

Ivy watched as the proprietor wiped his sweaty palms on his plaid flannel shirt.

"Well, that explains where he's been then." Tom relaxed a bit. "Scout's been working for me for the past few years. The hunting guide down the street recommended him for the job. Hasn't missed many days during that time. Except when he's gone hunting. Before now, he always let me know in advance if he wasn't coming in. He's a good employee. He likes the detail work. Sometimes, he takes animal parts that we don't use. Said he makes jewelry."

"How about his friends or a girlfriend? Have you met anyone he hangs out with?" asked Ivy.

"He pretty much keeps to himself. There's one guy that has come around here though. I think his name's Danny. A hunting buddy. I don't know who would have wanted to hurt Scout. But it's hard to say. You think you know somebody, but you don't really." The taxidermist puffed out his chest in an attempt to show off his importance to the young detective.

"Yeah," agreed Ivy, distractedly, wondering what Rex would think about the taxidermist. "One last question, where were you Tuesday?"

"Here in the shop. I have five bear rugs to repair by the end of the week. And without Scout, I have to work alone."

"Can anyone vouch for you?"

"No. But the shop was open Tuesday. I had to be here."

Well that didn't prove anything, thought Ivy, but she said, "Thanks. If you think of anything else that might be helpful, give me a call." She handed Tom Cathartes her card. She was thankful it only included her business contact information.

As Ivy left the dark room filled with empty, dead stares and its creepy, greasy, sweating overweight taxidermist, her mind cleared. It seems strange to hunt bears after they've been hibernating all winter, she thought. Wouldn't they be thin? Why shoot a skinny bear? Maybe she could learn more about bear hunting over dinner with Beau.

Chapter 8

A GUIDE TO HUNTING

Friday Morning

While Ivy met with Scout's employer, Rex hoped to learn more about Danny Darkfoot's whereabouts. He walked into the tidy front office of Varmint Outfitters, located at the other end of the block from the taxidermist and next door to Target Mart Gun Shop.

"Good Morning. I'm here to see Mr. Crockett," said Rex, as he extended his hand to a receptionist outfitted in a pink t-shirt and a desert camouflage patterned skirt.

"Is he expecting you?" the petite blonde asked.

"No, but I think he'll want to speak with me anyway," said Rex showing her his badge. He noted that she went to fetch Crockett from his office instead of calling him on the phone. As he waited, he glanced around at the walls covered with pictures of clients holding up trophy animals. A plant enthusiast himself, Rex just didn't understand the desire to kill animals. He did, however, acknowledge the role hunters played in keeping wildlife populations in check. After all, an over-sized herd of elk could destroy a thriving plant community!

Rex had just picked up a Varmint Outfitters' brochure from a glass coffee table when Boone Crockett stepped into the front office. He slipped the brochure into his jacket.

"Are you here to sign up for one of our trophy hunts, Detective?" boomed the big man with a bass voice. The grip of his paw nearly crushed Rex's hand when they shook hands. Boone Crockett sported an olive-green buttoned shirt, a red and black-checked wool vest, jeans, and cowboy boots. Ruddy cheeks popped out from a cinnamon-colored beard and mustache. Thick, matching hair and eyebrows topped piercing brown eyes. The man looked like he had just stepped from the cover of a Varmint Outfitters' brochure.

"Actually, I'm here on a different sort of hunt. I'm looking for a young Spokane Indian man. His name's Danny Darkfoot. He went missing Tuesday. His grandmother is worried about him. She told me he worked for you. I'm hoping you can help me find him."

"Let's see. Darkfoot? Young Indian lad?" said the big man contemplating. "I don't recall anyone named Darkfoot." He paused. "And he's only been missing three days you say? Hell, if he's a hunter, he's likely to be off in the woods for weeks. What's this fellow involved in that you cops are looking for him after only three days?"

Rex pulled out of his jacket the picture of Danny he had received from Winnie Milne. He stepped over to a picture on the wall. In the photograph, Danny Darkfoot and three other young men wearing Varmint Outfitter hats and hunting vests stretched out a dead black bear while a grinning hunter stood with a Remington rifle in hand and his boot on the bear's head. Rex held the smaller photo up next to the larger picture of the bear, hunter and guides.

"This sure looks like the same Danny Darkfoot I'm searching for," said Rex.

"Well now," admitted Boone, looking more closely at the photo of Danny. "I suppose it could be him. I contract with lots of freelance guides when we get busy. He could've been on one of our hunts. Anyway, I haven't seen him around here lately. Besides, I run a squeaky-clean operation. I wouldn't hire anyone in trouble with the cops."

"How about any of the other guides? Do you know anyone else who might know where Danny might be?" asked Rex.

"Can't say as I do," Boone replied testily. "But I tell you what. If he shows up around here, you'll be the first person I call."

Rex could see he wouldn't get much help from this surly guide. He thanked Crockett and left the outfitter's building to meet Ivy for lunch at Tofucious. The business was a Korean market for years in the neighborhood. Recently, it added a restaurant and was just two blocks away. He chose to make the short walk.

Rex was already sitting in a booth and trying to decipher the menu when Ivy arrived. He was thankful for the pictures because, based on their names, he couldn't tell what the dishes were.

"Be with you in a minute, Boss," said Ivy. She felt a strong urge to wash up after being in the taxidermy shop. She might even choose a vegetarian dish.

As she returned to the table, she spied Tom, the taxidermist, leaving out the market's front door with a large paper sack. Did he order take-out or was he stalking her, Ivy wondered suspiciously. She sat down and the waiter brought a second menu and glass of water. He informed his guests that the day's special was bibimbab, a boiled rice hash with meat and veggies.

"Is there anything with pasta?" Rex asked, longing for spaghetti Bolognese.

"You could try the kimchi noodle soup. It has noodles, but it doesn't have any meat."

"Make that two," said Ivy, echoing Rex's order.

After the waiter left, she leaned over the table and whispered, "Good choice sticking with the veggie option. I just saw the taxidermist leaving. Not sure if he was picking up or delivering."

Rex laughed. "Sounds like you're skeptical about the taxidermist. What did you learn about Scout Blueblood at the taxidermy shop?" he asked Ivy.

She recounted what Cathartes told her about Scout being an exemplary employee and confirmed that Tom also knew of Danny. "The place was kind of eerie. It felt like hundreds of eyes were staring at me," Ivy said, and involuntarily shuddered. "There was something odd about Cathartes too. That guy gave me goose bumps. He didn't give me any reason to think he would hurt Scout, but I checked if he had an alibi for Tuesday anyway. He said he was working alone in the shop."

"It sounds like he was more helpful than the hunting guide, anyway," said Rex. "Boone Crockett denied knowing Danny Darkfoot, but a photograph on the wall had Danny in the picture. When I asked him about it, Crockett told me Danny was likely a one-time, freelance guide."

"That's interesting. The taxidermist told me that the 'hunting guide' down the street recommended he hire Scout Blueblood. The only guide shop on the block is Varmint Outfitters."

"So, Crockett not only knows Danny Darkfoot, but is acquainted with Scout Blueblood well enough to give Cathartes a recommendation," mused Rex. "I wonder what kind of dirt Crockett's hiding in that squeaky-clean operation?"

Chapter 9

DEAD OR ALIVE?

Sunday Morning, Late April

Rex sat at his usual table by a fuschia-framed window in Cafe Noir participating in his favorite activities, drinking a Vatican and looking out the window while his mind drifted. It was his preferred method for analyzing a difficult homicide case. Cafe Noir served the best espresso in town, and the Vatican with a hint of Frangelico and cardamom always put the detective in a heavenly frame of mind to divine the intricacies of murder cases. The barista, Gina, always made it with a heart shape in the foam. Rex was sure she did it just for him.

It was Sunday morning. Today, Rex took a break from running. He had run the Bloomsday route, plus extra miles, yesterday as he compensated for lost training time. For some reason, O'Dendren and the others seemed to be taking the race more seriously the last few days. Rex turned toward the window and watched the churchgoers enter St. Ignatius Church next door. He wondered if it would help to stop by the church later and offer a prayer for speed and endurance. Surely there must be a patron saint of runners?

What he really needed help with was the Scout Blueblood case. Rex and Ivy didn't have much information yet. Tribal Chief Andy Blueblood and his officers had followed up with contacts on the reservation that might know if either Danny or Scout had resumed any drug activity. The tribal authorities had come up blank. According to Louie, the Cash Cow Casino manager, there wasn't any apparent tie to the casino. Except, Rex pondered, Scout was found outside by the dumpster, bloodied and possibly left for dead. Why there? Was there any significance to the location?

Chief Blueblood and his brother Andy both suspected a connection between Scout and Danny. And Danny disappeared about the same time Scout was attacked. Did Danny and Scout have a falling out? Did Danny assault his friend and then leave the area? Or did a similar fate befall Danny?

It would help if Rex could talk with Scout, but the young man was still comatose. It was easier solving a homicide case, mused Rex as he sipped the Frangelico-laced divine inspiration and gazed out the window. At least in those cases there would be a body of evidence. A good crime lab often found clues to the perpetrator on the remains. EMTs and medical professionals, in their efforts to save a person, usually destroyed evidence that a medical examiner would normally find on the deceased. Or, the evidence could only be accessed once a body was dead. But Scout was alive, and Rex fervently hoped the young man stayed that way. In Danny's case, the detective didn't have a body dead or alive.

So what had Rex learned? In addition to Danny going missing about the time Scout was assaulted, Danny had told his grandmother he was going hunting and would be gone a few days. He and Scout shared an interest in hunting. Danny, and possibly Scout, had worked for Varmint Outfitters. And, the Varmint Outfitters' owner had lied to Rex.

That reminded him. He pulled the Varmint Outfitters' brochure out of his jacket and laid it on the table. The cover featured a photo of the owner dressed in hunting gear atop a granite peak. He had one foot firmly planted on a big horn sheep carcass and a high-powered rifle casually slung across his shoulder. Beneath the picture was the name Boone A. Crockett. Inside the brochure, photos of big game the company specialized in tracking were splashed across the glossy pages. Short descriptions of the types of hunting excursions offered accompanied the pictures. Further details included photos and bios for the guides: Herb Vore, deer and elk specialist; Al Ces, moose specialist; and Alex Kamchatka, bear specialist. The brochure listed additional information covering hunting seasons, locations, equipment provided and prices. Big bucks indeed, thought the detective.

As Spokane's top homicide detective, Rex knew a great deal about human killers, but not much about animal hunting. He was a plant person. Plants and books filled his comfortable craftsman home while an informal garden accounted for most of the yard outside. He would have to ask Chief Blueblood if the chief knew anything about Varmint Outfitters. Maybe Tom's Taxidermy, too.

Chapter 10

Hunting Stories

Monday Morning, Late April

After Monday morning's briefing, Rex and Ivy met with Chief Blueblood. The chief didn't have any additional information about Varmint Outfitters or Tom's Taxidermy. "You might visit with Sheriff Wyatt," recommended the chief. "She can fill in the details on the hunting story you're interested in since the incident took place north of town and her department investigated."

Rex arranged for he and Ivy to meet the sheriff at the Ugly Mug Coffee Shop in Airway Heights, about 30 minutes west of Spokane. They also planned to rendezvous with Tribal Chief Andy Blueblood and go to Scout's apartment, which was near the casino and not far from the Ugly Mug. The detective hoped that even if they couldn't interview Scout, the young man's apartment still could provide them with clues.

Sheriff Wyatt and a deputy were waiting with welcoming cups of steaming coffee when the two detectives arrived. "Hi, Rex. I hear the chief is letting you venture out of town," kidded Wyatt, as she stood and shook Rex's right hand and deftly crossed arms to place a hot cup in his left. "This is Deputy Mark Dillon." She nodded in the deputy's direction.

"Nice to see you again, too, Sheriff," deadpanned Rex. "Meet my partner, Detective Ivy Lizei."

"Pleased to meet you, Detective Lizei. Chief Blueblood finally decided to give Rex some help, huh?" The sheriff called out to her assistant in the outer office to bring tea when Ivy shook her head no to the proffered coffee and mouthed a silent plea for tea.

Sheriff Wyatt sat down and continued in a different vein. "All kidding aside. What can we do for you two? The chief said you're working on a case

41

that might have a connection to a hunting accident last fall." She went on, "And while you're here, maybe you can update me on the incident at the casino that Chief Blueblood mentioned. Because the assault took place at the tribal casino, our office is taking a backseat to the tribal police even though the casino is not on the reservation."

Rex explained that the two cases might be related. He updated the sheriff and deputy about what little they had learned about Scout Blueblood. Rex shared his suspicion about a link between Scout Blueblood and Varmint Outfitters. The link involved Danny Darkfoot, whose whereabouts were still unknown. No missing person report had been filed, but the grandmother had shared her concern with Rex and Ivy during their visit with her. County law enforcement might want to be on the lookout for him.

"Danny Darkfoot. The name's familiar. As I recall, he was one of the guides on the hunt you're curious about," mentioned the sheriff.

"Boone Crockett acted like he didn't know Danny when I interviewed him last week," said Rex. "Then he backtracked when I pointed out Danny in a picture on the wall. Crockett said Danny could have been a one-time freelance guide.

"When people lie, it makes me wonder what else they aren't telling me," Rex continued. "I don't have anything on Crockett, and he wasn't exactly talkative. He talked to you during the hunting investigation. What did you learn about Varmint Outfitters?"

"It was a difficult case," admitted Wyatt. "We even brought the FBI in because the victim was a Korean businessman. He didn't have any hunting experience but had lots of money and wanted to shoot a trophy bear in the 'American wilderness.'

"Two of Varmint Outfitters' guides and another client were with Moon Ye Jun, the victim, when he was shot. They all swore the shot was self-inflicted when Moon slipped while crossing a stream. The bullet entered just below the heart. It matched with the Remington 700 .30-06 the client was using. Varmint Outfitters actually owned the rifle, but it was checked out to Moon for the hunt."

"The newspaper article mentioned there was another client and guide. Where were they?" asked Rex.

"The hunting party included the Korean, two other clients, three guides and Crockett. Darkfoot was one of the guides. We interviewed them all separately and their stories matched up. Each client was with a guide. The other guide and client were a quarter of a mile away. Crockett was at the camp.

"The guides administered first aid and carried the victim out of the woods. They called for medical assistance when they got to the trailhead. About five hours passed from the time the victim was shot until he got to the hospital. He died on the way.

"My deputies hiked back to the scene with one of the guides. They didn't find anything at the site where the victim was shot or at the hunting camp to dispute the stories. With all of the witnesses' accounts matching and no evidence to prove otherwise, it was determined to be an unfortunate hunting accident. Crockett has tried to keep the incident quiet. He's afraid it will hurt his business."

"So, Crockett and Danny were there. Who else? One of them didn't happen to be Scout Blueblood?" Rex asked.

"It's been a few months. I'll have to pull the file and send you the names. Wasn't Blueblood, though. I would have recognized the name."

"Strange that they waited so long to call for help," commented Ivy.

"Cell service is poor in that area," Sheriff Wyatt replied.

One of many wilderness hazards, thought Rex. He thanked the sheriff and deputy for their help. "Let us know if you see or hear anything regarding Danny's whereabouts, too," he added.

"Say 'hi' to your boss for me," responded Wyatt. "I hope his nephew is better soon."

Rex hoped so, also. He had numerous questions, and it would help if they could talk with Scout.

After saying their good-byes, the two Spokane detectives drove down a backstreet and parked by an older, multi-story apartment building. There, they met Tribal Chief Andy Blueblood outside of apartment 204.

"This is it," said Andy. "I'm sure Scout wouldn't be happy about us searching through his apartment but if it helps brings justice to whoever beat him up, he's probably okay with it. Fortunately, his mom had a key."

The small apartment was clean and retained few furnishings. It smelled of sage. A compound bow and a quiver of arrows hung prominently from hooks on one wall. A large painting adorned another wall. The artwork featured a large black bear standing on its hind legs. Young braves on horses surrounded the bear. One brave appeared to be speaking to the bear. Stars filled a night sky behind the bear and braves. Jewelry making tools sat on a shelf above a worktable. Bear claws and teeth, porcupine quills, antlers, bones, wires, and leather strips filled jars and baskets on the shelf and table. A partially constructed necklace made of braided leather and bear claws lay on the table.

"He's a talented artist," said Ivy softly, touching the necklace with a gloved hand. "He seems to have an affinity for bears."

"Yes," said Andy. "Scout showed an interest in art at an early age. He sharpened his skills working with our elders over the years. The bear is his spirit animal, providing him guidance and protection."

A small pile of mail sat on the counter, but otherwise they found little in the way of a paper trail in the apartment. "Looks like Scout uses his phone for everything. No paper calendars, address books or other clues," Rex observed.

Before they left the apartment, Tribal Chief Blueblood grabbed a Pendleton blanket from the bed and a sage bundle. He would take them to the hospital and visit his son.

Chapter 11

TRAINING DAY

Monday Afternoon, Last Week of April

On Monday afternoon, Rex and Ivy were 20,000 feet above the Cascade Mountains and on their way to Seattle for the interagency training. Ivy peered out the window of the plane at the snow-capped peaks and forests below. Miles of impenetrable trees and cold rock spread below. A week had passed and they were no closer to solving the case.

Between working on the case and training for Bloomsday, Ivy hadn't seen much of Beau Hunter lately. She hoped to free up more time after Sunday's race. She still hadn't introduced him to Rex and her other colleagues. She wondered what Rex would think of Beau. She looked over at her partner whose distinctive Roman nose was buried deep in a book.

"What are you reading?" Ivy asked, hoping to start a conversation.

"*Ulysses* by James Joyce. It's a literary classic."

"What's it about?"

Rex reminded himself that Ivy's exemplary qualities more than made up for her mettlesome nature. "It's a novel about a day in the life of Leopold Bloom. It follows him and his encounters throughout Dublin, Ireland during the early 20th Century. The story is constructed much like Homer's *Odyssey*," he explained patiently. "In both stories, the hero experiences a series of adventures as he journeys toward home. In Bloom's case, all of his adventures take place on a single day – June 16. In Ireland, June 16 is celebrated as Bloomsday."

"Wow! Another Bloomsday! How do they celebrate?"

"People dress up as characters in the story. They visit the various locations where Leopold Bloom journeyed throughout the day. They read and celebrate together by drinking in pubs," explained Rex, thinking if he was going to participate in one Bloomsday, why not two? Maybe O'Dendren could recommend an Irish pub in Spokane?

"Oh," said Ivy becoming quiet. Although she could reference plants by their Latin names and discuss them endlessly with her partner, she felt intimidated by his knowledge of literary classics. Was there a literary classic about plants she could read?

The plane started descending toward Seattle. Ivy looked out the window at coniferous forests flowing down the mountains then opening into an urban area, flush with verdant parks and lush landscapes. The skyscrapers of the Emerald City and sparkling waters of Puget Sound came into view as the pilot reminded passengers to sit and fasten seat belts. No matter how often she crossed the state, the stark vegetative differences between the dry east side and the wet westside of Washington amazed her. Ivy relished the diversity.

After landing, the two detectives rode a shuttle bus to their hotel, The Rainy Seasons, which was close to the Federal Building downtown. The Federal Bureau of Investigation was hosting the training, scheduled to begin early the following morning. After checking in at the hotel, the pair made time that afternoon for a run, navigating the congested streets of Seattle.

"More practice for Bloomsday," panted Ivy as they zig-zagged through the throng of pedestrians carrying umbrellas and packages along the waterfront. A light drizzle moved in and kept the runners comfortably cool. Spring started earlier in Seattle than it did in Spokane. New green leaves on trees gave meaning to the name Emerald City. Azaleas and rhododendrons were in full bloom, their bushes tucked into landscaping nestled beside the glass and steel skyscrapers.

Although not a fan of crowds, Rex worried more about the killer Seattle hills. By the time they had wound through 7.46 miles of city streets and up and down the steep hills, he was plotting revenge on Ivy and O'Dendren. He needed coffee! Fortunately, Seattle boasted more coffee shops than rainy days in a year.

His 4 a.m. trip to the Spokane Airport, the flight and shuttle ride through traffic, combined with the exertion of running Seattle hills, left Rex tired and exhausted. He wasn't looking forward to sitting in a classroom for eight hours the next day. After a dinner of linguine with clams, a short walk, and a review of the afternoon's emails, he fell asleep in the middle of chapter eleven of *Ulysses*.

Ivy, despite not consuming anywhere near as much caffeine as her colleague, couldn't sleep. She called Beau just to hear his soothing voice. This was the first time they wouldn't see each other for a whole week since they met a few months ago, and she missed him already. He told her about tracing the horse carcass in the Selkirk Mountains to a group of poachers operating in Northeast Washington and North Idaho. Ivy recalled Rex telling her about the Wolverine Case he had worked on years ago. It also involved poachers from North Idaho. In that case, a pair of backwoods brothers killed a famous anti-fur advocate after he ratted them out for illegally hunting endangered species of animals.

"Forest criminals are more common in these parts than you would think," Beau explained. "Everything from timber thieves stealing cedar to hoodlums poaching pelts. Some of these cases involve hundreds of thousands of dollars and serious weapons while the culprits usually don't do any substantial time."

Ivy told Beau about her visit to Tom's Taxidermy Shop and the creepy sensation she experienced interacting with Tom Cathartes. It felt comforting to confide in Beau.

"Cathartes been on the department's watch list for years. He's suspected of buying and selling threatened and endangered animal parts," said Beau. "We just haven't been able to catch him yet. He's as slippery as a wet goose."

"Have you been in his shop lately?" asked Ivy, thinking of the sage grouse.

"Did you see something that made you suspicious?"

"I suppose he can't be arrested just for being beastly," she reflected. "But he did admit a stuffed bird on display was a sage grouse. Aren't sage grouse endangered?"

"Here in Washington, yes. Species protection is different in Idaho though. We're practically on the border here in Spokane. Unless we can prove the grouse came from Washington, there's not much we can do," Beau explained.

If Ivy had her way, Cathartes would be endangered.

The next morning, Rex woke early and headed toward the waterfront. Luckily, he had noticed a petite cafe, Lotto Gelato, while walking the previous evening. He figured an Italian cafe was a likely place to find an excellent cappuccino. His detective skills did not fail him. After choosing a small table by a window, he settled in with a cappuccino and a warm, buttery brioche with strawberry jam. It would have to last him through the day. Breaks during government trainings usually consisted of weak coffee and dry, day-old pastries.

Rex was scheduled to participate in a Cross Cultural Issues class that morning while Ivy would sit through an Electronic Information Sharing course. During the 29 years Rex worked in law enforcement, the senior detective occasionally collaborated with some of the other agencies represented at the training. Today's class incorporated a wider spectrum of policing. In addition to municipal and county law enforcement, state, federal and tribal agencies were present. There were at least twenty federal agencies – everything from the Bureau of Alcohol, Tobacco and Firearms to the U.S. Customs and Border Protection. A veritable alphabet soup served during the conference. Rex wondered what the law enforcement officer to criminal ratio was in the U.S. currently.

The week progressed with training as dry as the pastries. The information was valuable, Rex knew, but he longed to get back on a real case. On Thursday, all agency trainees would participate in an anti-trafficking round table to discuss the latest developments regarding trafficking and what resources their agencies could offer to deal with the problem. Ironically, the State Patrol had raised the trafficking issue. At least he could look forward to the field trip to the Port of Seattle on Friday, the final morning of the training.

Each day after the classroom training, Rex and Ivy stretched their legs on Seattle's downtown hills and traded stories from their respective workshops. Most evenings, they poured over homework or caught up on communications from their cases back in Spokane. At least a couple of nights, they met up with training colleagues in the hotel hospitality room where they discussed workshop topics and traded stories before going out to explore Seattle's many restaurant options.

After nearly a week of running hills, Rex began to feel more confident about the upcoming Bloomsday Race. And Chief Blueblood would be pleased that Rex had stretched his people skills too. The introverted detective had made a few friends among the other agency law enforcement personnel. He was surprised to find that one of the workshop instructors, FBI Special Agent Ursula Maidger, knew Molly Murrow from the reporter's early television days in Seattle. Maidger was the first Black, and coincidentally the first woman, Special Agent in Charge of the Seattle FBI Field Office. Her sharp wit and intellect reminded Rex of Molly. He was looking forward to returning home. Just one more day of training.

On the final day, training participants from the many agencies met at the Port of Seattle's waterfront for a field trip of the Port's maritime facilities. It was an opportunity to see many federal, state and local agencies working together to support the region's economic and trade activity. The Port connected the region's farmers and manufacturers to world markets. More than six million cargo containers moved through the Port annually.

Large orange cranes reached skyward, rivaling the height of small skyscrapers. The cranes loaded and unloaded shipping containers from ships exceeding the length of three football fields and often stacked several stories high with more containers buried deep in the bowels of the large vessels. The metal containers arrived and left by truck and train. The Port was a hubbub of activity. Trucks honked and beeped, workers shouted and containers clanged against each other. Seagulls dive-bombed Native American fishermen setting their nets nearby.

Rex and Ivy learned that the Port of Seattle Police worked regularly with three city police departments, the King County Sheriff's Office and multiple state and federal agencies. The U.S. Customs and Border Protection agency oversaw cargo inspections and worked with a slew of partner agency specialists ranging from agriculturalists to zoologists.

Before finishing their tour, the attendees climbed aboard a U.S. Coast Guard Legend-class cutter. Rex was thrilled. Despite the many lakes around Spokane, crime-fighting in the Lilac City didn't allow for many opportunities to be on a 418-foot stealth ship that could travel over 28 knots, commanded anti-surface weapon capability, and could provide naval gunfire support.

On the plane back to Spokane, Ivy and Rex discussed the Port tour. She planned to tell Beau about the salmon habitat restoration being done as part of the Port of Seattle's terminal construction along the Duwamish Waterway. He would appreciate the efforts to save the iconic, yet threatened, Northwest fish.

Rex remarked on the complexity and many levels of agency cooperation that took place to make one of the state's largest economic engines, the Port, function. But the biggest surprise for him was learning that Washington was a top exporter of white wheat – the best kind for making pasta noodles. After a week of training for Bloomsday by running hills, he was ready to move onto carbo-loading and a big bowl of Bolognese!

Chapter 12

RACE PREP

Saturday, First Week of May

It was the day before the big race. Downtown Spokane bustled with people picking up race packets at the convention center and visiting the local attractions. Hotel vans shuttled back and forth to the airport picking up and delivering world-class and amateur athletes alike. The population of the city grew by a third for Bloomsday weekend. Hotels, motels, B&Bs and many residents' spare bedrooms were booked months ago. Bar and restaurant owners anticipated one of their busiest weekends of the year. It was impossible to imagine spring in Spokane without the buzz surrounding Bloomsday.

A warm sun shone on the racers and their families in Riverfront Park, next to the Convention Center. The sound of children yelling and laughing filled the air. They climbed the Paul Bunyon-sized red wagon and fed candy wrappers to the garbage goat, an interactive, metal sculpture. A blur of brightly colored running shoes and gear competed with the spring blooms for visual attention. The scent of lilacs filled the air. The Spokane River wound through the city and roared over the falls in the park. It sent up sprays of cold, mountain-snowmelt water to splash delighted viewers on the pedestrian bridge spanning the river.

Mayor Sammy Prosciutto smiled as he looked out his fifth-floor office window overlooking Riverfront Park and the many visitors. Spokane excelled at hosting large events and maintained many beautiful parks. The Lilac Bloomsday Race, in the heart of the city, attracted attention and tourist dollars to Spokane. And attention and dollars were dear to the mayor's heart. He had a busy day planned – engaging in media events, meeting with visiting dignitaries, speaking at a Rotary luncheon – all part of promoting his beloved city. And that evening, he would speak at a carbo-loading, spaghetti dinner hosted by the Spokane Italian American Club. Mayor Sammy Prosciutto was its most honorable and well-fed member.

Sergeant O'Dendren and Ivy had offered to pick up race packets for the Spokane Police Department's Corporate Cup team, the Flatfoots. Rex, instead, spent that sunny afternoon planting and weeding in his garden. He was glad to only deal with the crowds on race day. Oh, and he was thankful for the race's prerequisite spaghetti dinner.

As prominent members of the Italian American Club, the Begonia family played an integral role in the annual dinner. Mama Begonia was famous for her spaghetti Bolognese and grocer Papa Begonia supplied the fixings. The whole family helped cook, serve, clean up or eat the dinner. Even if Rex didn't plan to be there for the carbo-loading, he still would attend the dinner.

Ivy waited for Sergeant Phil O'Dendren by the metal sculpture of Bloomsday runners in Riverfront Park. An anonymous someone had adorned them with past year's race t-shirts in a rainbow of colors. The burly sergeant's young son Liam and daughter Mary ran a few feet ahead of their father as the group approached the meeting spot with Ivy.

"Did you recruit more runners for the team?" Ivy teased, nodding toward her colleague's children.

"Look at my shoes! I have new sneakers!" shouted Liam. He wiggled his skinny, six-year-old leg with excitement. The attached foot, covered in a bright red running shoe, waved happily.

"Ooh. Those look fast," exclaimed Ivy, examining the shoe while Liam hopped on the other foot.

"And they're sneaky," Liam whispered confidentially to Ivy.

"Liam and Mary are here to pick up packets for Team O'Dendren," said the Sergeant. "Wendy's taking some of the kids. She's been doing this for twenty years, sometimes as a runner; sometimes with a stroller or walking with the kids. This is Liam's first year. They'll be tough competition for the Flatfoots." He smiled proudly.

Sergeant O'Dendren and his wife Wendy had five children between the ages of three and thirteen. Ivy wondered if the O'Dendren family participated in Hoopfest, the city's three-on-three basketball tournament, too. Maybe they were growing their own basketball team.

"A few more years, we'll be ready for Hoopfest," laughed O'Dendren, reading her mind. "Let's go get those race packets."

With Liam leading the way, they crossed the park and joined the swarm of people pouring into the convention center, up the escalators and descending on the registration area. A rainbow of lilac-colored balloons arched over the entryway. Tables signed with age ranges and sections of the alphabet ringed the room. Volunteers in purple t-shirts crossed names off lists and handed out bags with race numbers and swag to each registrant. Ivy retrieved packets for her team while O'Dendren picked up packets for the O'Dendren clan.

Mission accomplished, they wandered through the trade show. Vendors hawked running gear, energy drinks, massage chairs, and more. The O'Dendrens munched on free chocolate-covered mini donuts. Ivy bought a rain jacket and two pairs of anti-blister socks from an outdoor sporting exhibitor. The salesman gave her a complimentary *Pocket Emergency Survival Guide*. That looks handy, she thought. On a whim, she asked for copies for her team members.

The biggest race sponsor, Ruddy Bulldog, dominated one corner of an extra-large open exhibit area with a truck loaded with cans of energy drinks. Here, more than a dozen of the national and international elite runners and their coaches lounged on sofas and chairs or sat at tables and signed autographs. A few of them stretched and flexed their leg muscles.

Liam rushed up to two tall, lanky Kenyans. "Are you a fast runner? Can I have your autograph? Do you want my autograph? I'm a fast runner," he said looking up expectantly into a dark face with a broad white smile and twinkling eyes. The Kenyans laughed.

"Well, we'll know tomorrow who is the fastest runner," one of them said amiably. He signed Liam's race bib, then handed a pen to the boy to sign a rubber wristband that the Kenyan wore. His friend did the same.

"Ab – sko?" Liam sounded out the words written on his race bib.

"Absko and Sokoro. Sokoro means the lucky one," answered the man's companion. "Good luck to you, in the race little fast one," said the Kenyan.

"Don't forget to say 'thank you,'" Sergeant O'Dendren reminded his son.

Meanwhile, Ivy and Mary stood in front of a table with female runners. Ivy asked the woman at the end of the table for an autograph for shy Mary. The muscular woman with blue eyes and a tight blonde ponytail signed her name to Mary's race bib without smiling. Beside her, a large, middle-aged man in a tracksuit spoke animatedly in a foreign language with a younger man. Both men sported thick, dark beards.

Ivy noticed a tattoo of a bear wearing a starred hat on the man's hand. Must be the Russians, she thought as Liam and the sergeant rejoined them.

"Hey, O'Dendren!" A loud voice boomed behind them.

"What in blazes?" the sergeant sputtered, recognizing the voice and turning around to face Fire Chief Billy Blaize and two of his firefighters.

"Better not spend all your money," joked the fire chief. "You'll need a Benjamin to settle our bet after tomorrow's race."

"You're sounding overconfident, Blaize."

"Yeah, it's easy to be confident when the competition is flatfooted."

Snickering erupted from the firefighters.

While the firemen and the sergeant joked, Ivy and the O'Dendren children wandered over to the Bloomsday Master Gardeners' booth. Vases of lilacs poked up between books and pamphlets about xeriscaping, proper pruning, organic vegetable growing and more. Liam and Mary plunged their hands into a worm and compost bin. The volunteers offered them complimentary seed packets of Scarlet Runner Beans and small bags of worm castings.

"Ooh. Slimy," exclaimed Liam.

Mary grimaced and wiped her hand on the back of Liam's shirt.

By the time they left the convention center, the O'Dendren children wore chocolate on their faces and compost on their clothes. They held race packets in one hand and purple balloons in the other. "It's time I get these two home," said Sergeant O'Dendren. "They have a big day tomorrow. Our oldest daughter is making a spaghetti dinner at home so Wendy and I can join you at the Italian American Club. See you later this evening."

Ivy had just enough time to stop by her father Joe Lizei's house and tell him about the training in Seattle and then clean up before Beau arrived to take her to the dinner. She was nervous. She would be introducing him to her partner and mentor, Detective Rex Begonia, and to Chief Blueblood, as well as her other colleagues.

Chapter 13

A DELICACY

Saturday Night

The Italian American Club's spaghetti dinner on the eve of the Bloomsday Race offered the city's prominent citizens a chance to mingle with international and national visitors and the running elite. Delegations from Kenya, Ethiopia, Britain, Russia and Australia were there, as well as top runners from the Boston and New York marathons.

Bets were on the Kenyans to win the men's division again this year, while the up-and-coming Russian was favored to challenge last year's winner in the women's division. Army veteran Jean Patton held the record in the wheelchair division and was expected to win again. Mayor Sammy Prosciutto had invited the director of the Bloomsday Race Foundation and some of the international and national dignitaries to sit at the head table.

Crystal chandeliers sparkled and lit up the room set for 500 diners. Forty years of framed race posters featuring the work of local artists lined the walls of the fancy Davenport Hotel ballroom. Light purple, linen tablecloths and sprays of lilacs in trophy-shaped, crystal bowls adorned the tables. Somehow the mix of luxury and sport worked for the evening decor.

As a leader in the community, Chief Barney Blueblood attended the dinner even though he wasn't running in the race. He sat with his officers, the members of the Flatfoot team. Twenty feet away and within eyesight sat Fire Chief Billy Blaize and the firefighters' team, The Heat.

Rex looked around the room. He recognized many of Spokane's leading citizens – Judge Rudy Marconi, Manito Park's Head Gardener Toni Fritts, developer Wes Larch, the Bloomenthals, the Dentons, and Ginger Wild, the artist who designed this year's race poster. He hoped to see a certain sandy brown-haired reporter. He finally spied KRUM-TV reporter Molly

Murrow. She was at a media table with other reporters and camera crews from ESPN, Sports Northwest and other local stations. Maybe he would wait until she wasn't surrounded by cameras before he said "hello."

"This is my friend Beau Hunter," Ivy announced cheerfully, as she and her new boyfriend arrived at the table. "Beau, this is Chief Barney Blueblood and his wife Beatrice, Phil and Wendy O'Dendren, Bruce and Carol Hemlock and of course my partner at the department, Detective Rex Begonia."

"What? Oh," said Rex turning around. "This is the beau?"

"Just Beau. Pleased to meet you," he said shaking Rex's hand. "Ivy's told me how much she's learned working with you." He then nodded and shook hands with the others, although he couldn't remember all their names.

Meanwhile, Rex scrutinized Beau the way a father would. The young man seemed pleasant and self-assured. He wore a slim-fitting suit and narrow tie; his sandy-colored hair was neatly trimmed. What had Ivy said he did? Work in the woods?

Officer Hemlock asked Beau whether he planned to run in Bloomsday. The race dominated the discussion while they passed baskets of hot breadsticks and devoured Caesar salads.

Rex anticipated the main event – steaming bowls of spaghetti Bolognese – a true delicacy! Since this was a carbo-loading party, he planned to do some heavy lifting.

Chief Blueblood asked Sergeant O'Dendren if he felt confident about the Flatfoots' chances beating Blaize's firefighters.

"Losing Silva was a blow, but we added Rex," said O'Dendren. "Hopefully, he and Ivy kept training while in Seattle."

"I'm counting on you," the chief lightheartedly reminded them.

"We ran every day. Nothing but hills," boasted Ivy.

"Killer hills," said Rex, starting to get suspicious. "Is there something I don't know about? What do you mean counting on us, Chief?"

Sergeant O'Dendren's face took on the color of Bolognese sauce. "Sorry Rex. I didn't tell you. There's more than our reputation riding on the race. Chief Blaize challenged us and, well, we couldn't turn down the challenge."

"You bet money on the race?" asked Rex, incredulously.

"O'Dendren did but Blaize and I just have a friendly competition going between the police and fire departments," said Chief Blueblood. "If the Flatfoots win, the firefighters will wash your police vehicles."

"And if we lose?"

"Not going to happen. But if we do, we wash their fire trucks," O'Dendren admitted sheepishly.

Before the conversation could go any further, Ivy quickly turned to Rex and said, "Beau's solved the case with the horse carcass found in the Selkirks. Turns out it wasn't devil worshippers or mushroom gangs."

Everyone looked at Ivy and Beau. Now it was Beau's turn to feel self-conscious.

O'Dendren took the baton from Ivy. "What kind of a case was it?" he asked the young wildlife officer.

"Poaching. There's been an uptick in illegal black bear hunting over the last couple of years," said Beau. "The horse carcass was used as bait. Bear-baiting is legal in neighboring Idaho but not here in Washington. We're so close to the border that some of the Idaho hunters forget where they are when they're out in the woods."

"They don't use GPS or maps?" asked Beatrice Blueblood.

"Some of them aren't the sharpest axes in the woodshed," Beau answered.

"I didn't realize hunting black bear was so popular," posed Rex, who thought most reasonable people would prefer gardening and eating vegetables. "Do people eat bear meat, or is the hunting mostly for sport?"

"Some do," answered Beau. "It's considered a delicacy in Asian cultures. In Korea and China, people also use the bile and gall bladder for medicine and the gall bladder as an aphrodisiac. They can fetch thousands of dollars on the black market. It's more valuable than gold.

"Black bears in Asia have been hunted to the point of being endangered. We still have a healthy population here in the States. But in the Northwest, we have to watch out for smugglers. It's illegal to sell black bear parts internationally. Most of the trade with Asian countries takes place through our West Coast ports, which poses an opportunity for criminals wanting to tap into the black bear black market."

Rex wondered if Molly would consider a bear gall bladder an aphrodisiac. Just the thought of it made him uncomfortable.

"Bear meat is important for indigenous cultures, too," explained Chief Blueblood. "It's been part of our diet for centuries. We also use the fur, teeth, and claws. You probably noticed Scout's artwork when you visited his apartment with my brother. The black bear is his spirit animal. It not only protects him, it inspires his work."

Did the black bear protect the young man while outside the casino, wondered Rex. At least Scout was still alive.

The conversation transpired through the course of the dinner. By the time the diners had moved on to a dessert of gelato and biscotti served with the Davenport's house coffee, Mayor Sammy Prosciutto summoned Chief Blueblood to the table of dignitaries. Rex, who had also ordered an after-dinner espresso, watched as the mayor introduced the police chief to the out-of-town visitors. The mayor liked to make visitors feel important. That made him feel important too. Rex observed the introductions unfold from afar and just knew the mayor was planning some special job for the police department.

"What was that about?" Rex asked when the chief returned to the table.

"Mayor Prosciutto wants us to provide extra protection for our foreign visitors while they're in town," answered the chief.

"Have there been any threats?" asked Ivy, concerned.

"No. Nothing other than the usual trash talking between competitors. The mayor just wants to show respect to our visitors."

"Who's the bear of a guy with the dark beard and mustache? He gave you a menacing look," said Rex.

"Yeah, I noticed that too. He's the Russian husband and coach for Misha Middendorff. Misha is favored to win the women's division. His name's Mikhail Middendorff. Maybe he had a run-in with the Russian police and doesn't like law enforcement. We'll watch him extra carefully," Barney Blueblood said with his signature friendly smile.

"Well, it's been a delightful evening of carbo-loading and visiting, but Wendy and I have to put the O'Dendren team to bed. We'll see the rest of you Flatfoots in the morning. Meet at 8:30 a.m. by City Hall. We'll walk from there to the corporate cup start area," said Sergeant O'Dendren.

"Oh wait! Before everyone leaves, here are your race packets," Ivy said hurriedly, as she fumbled for them under her chair. "Check it out! I even scored some free *Pocket Emergency Survival Guides* at the trade show."

Rex didn't think he needed a *Pocket Emergency Survival Guide* to get through the race. But one never knew. He tried to catch Molly Murrow's attention before leaving, but she was busy chatting with a handsome thirty-something man wearing a *Runner's World* press pass. The competition. Well, it would be survival of the fittest and this old man had conquered some killer hills recently.

Chapter 14

RACE DAY

Sunday

Rex rose early on race day. The hardest part of this race might be forgoing his morning coffee, he thought ruefully. It was a tough choice, but he wanted to avoid the need to use the port a-potties along the seven-and-a-half mile race route. He checked the weather. It looked promising. Last night's rain clouds had disappeared. Sunshine and temperatures in the mid to upper 50s were forecast for the time of the race. The birds were singing. New green leaves emerged on the deciduous trees. Except for the lack of coffee, it was a perfect morning for the race.

Usually, Rex preferred quiet in the morning, but now he turned on the stereo and played the theme song from the movie *Rocky* on repeat. For today, he would be the Italian Stallion. He alternated between humming and singing as he washed and shaved. The reflection in the mirror revealed a middle-aged man with a prominent nose, kind eyes and dark, wavy hair, graying slightly. Would Molly consider him attractive, he wondered. At least he was back in shape. Ouch! A nick drew blood. Blood on Bloomsday – a bad omen.

He pulled on his running shorts and a t-shirt. Ivy had ordered the shirts printed special for The Flatfoots. Rex shook his head with disdain as he looked at a caricature of an early twentieth-century policeman running with huge, floppy feet and the team's name below the figure. He preferred a more sophisticated appearance. He pinned on his race number and set his running shoes by the door. After stretching, eating a light breakfast and going to the bathroom for what seemed like the thousandth time in an effort to avoid the port a-potties, Rex left home to meet up with his teammates downtown.

Ivy and the others were already at City Hall when Rex arrived.

"Everybody ready?" asked O'Dendren, while looking over his gathered teammates to assess that shoes were tied and everyone had their race bib. "This is a big day. We're going to show this town what the boys and girls in blue are made of."

They jogged to the designated start area for the corporate cup runners on Riverside Avenue. Already, runners, walkers and wheelchair racers packed shoulder-to-shoulder into their starting sections, which were color-coded and determined by expected finish times. The corporate cup teams wore white, personalized race bibs and were positioned near the front of the pack. The positioning gave the elite racers an advantage by allowing them to break free of the crowd. But a chip in the race bib recorded individual times from start to finish and negated the need for every racer to be positioned at the front of crowd. The technology was a significant factor in managing a race of more than 50,000 people.

Behind the corporate cup section, groups in brown, green, yellow, orange, blue, purple, and red race bibs jostled excitedly. Music blared overhead from large speakers set up near the start on each street. Racers nudged into position, jumped up and down to keep warm and gabbed with their neighbors while waiting for the 9 a.m. start. A few of the racers, running just for fun, were dressed in costumes. A Spiderman, ballerinas and a T-Rex stood out in the crowd. There was even a runner dressed as a pancake! A black bear in red, high-top, Converse sneakers stared at Rex navigating toward the corporate cup section.

Others, heading for the rear of the race pack, joked about having to walk so far to the back of the crowd that they'd be tired by the time they returned to the starting line. Beach balls and tortillas flew through the air while sweatshirts landed on trees to drape ceremoniously as runners ditched extra layers of clothing. TV cameras caught the action. A news helicopter hovered overhead. The streets resembled rivers of color with thousands of racers in bright running gear waiting for the start gun to fire.

Rex felt anxious to move and break free from the confines of the crowd. He could see the firefighters in their fire engine-red t-shirts about twenty feet ahead in the throng. They spotted the police team, too, and grinned.

"Hey, Flatfoots, eat our dust!" one of them shouted, taunting loud enough to be heard over the music blaring from speakers.

Rex silently vowed to overtake the firefighters.

Ivy yelled back, "Hosers!"

The Star-Spangled Banner and O Canada flowed from the podium. The racers cheered. A gun fired. The official Lilac Bloomsday Race commenced as the racers surged forward in a burst of color.

Elite runners quickly broke from the colorful tsunami of surging adrenaline streaming westward along Riverside Avenue. For the first mile, the Flatfoots stayed close together and kept in sight of the firefighters. It seemed to Ivy that her short legs forced her to run twice as fast as her colleagues to keep pace with them.

They ran through the historic Browne's Addition neighborhood, where residents and their guests lounged on porches and decks, already having started the day's partying. The onlookers waved to the racers and cheered them along. Some homes sported a history of Bloomsday t-shirts hanging along lines strung across porches and fences. Others blasted music from giant speakers which, along with the pounding of thousands of feet, seemed to rock the street and sidewalk.

The racers soon passed the first of the live bands playing along the race route and then headed downhill. At least a dozen bands, everything from rock-n-roll to singing nuns, were scattered along the route to provide entertainment for the competitors and the many spectators lining the roads. Volunteers in lilac-colored t-shirts staffed water stations. EMTs and on-duty police also worked the race route.

After the first mile, Rex hit his stride. He felt strong – like the Italian Stallion. Of course, the route had been flat or downhill so far. It was mostly uphill between the second and fourth miles. Near mile three, he spotted one of the young firefighters ducking into a port a-potty. This is where experience and not drinking caffeine in the morning makes a difference, Rex thought satisfactorily. Although, he and his teammates had separated, he could still see O'Dendren. Ivy was somewhere up ahead of course.

Rex passed the Spokane Falls Community College and headed downhill toward TJ Meenach Bridge, where it spanned the Spokane River downstream from Riverfront Park. As he ran down the hill, he could see across the river to where the route took a sharp right turn, then headed straight up Doomsday Hill. Already, the elite runners neared the top of the almost three-quarter mile section of Pettit Drive. The most difficult part of the race, Doomsday Hill, often separated the winners from the runners-up and featured an eight-foot, costumed vulture waiting for his victims to fall from the race.

Rex crossed the bridge and mentally readied himself for the hill. This is where the carb reserves would come in handy. A loud shriek interrupted his thoughts.

Turning toward the sound, Rex spied a group of people running away from the river. O'Dendren heard and saw the commotion too. Both men switched gears, bolting toward the screaming bystanders and away from the crowded race route.

Halfway up Doomsday Hill, Ivy missed the disturbance behind her. She was in her Zen space and focused only on the race. The sound of thousands of feet pounding on the concrete created a rhythm, helping to carry her up the long, steep hill. She did it! She crested the hill and passed the ominous vulture. The rest of the route was mostly flat. But for Ivy, this was the hardest part of the race. The exertion spent thus far started to take its toll. The distance between mile markers seemed to stretch farther than a mile. At last, the courthouse came into view and she knew the finish was nearby. The only teammates she saw were Hemlock and Pine. Ivy hoped the others were close behind. The finish line – one last push!

After nearly collapsing across the finish line, Ivy connected with her two teammates near City Hall. For several minutes, they looked around for Rex and Sergeant O'Dendren, but didn't see them anywhere. The flowing crowd of race finishers eventually swept up the three Flatfoots and carried them toward the tables where volunteers handed out lime green t-shirts to exhausted and exuberant competitors.

An on-duty officer approached Ivy at the t-shirt table and pulled her aside. "Detective Lizei. Chief Blueblood thought I might find you here. He wants you to grab your gear and head over the north side of TJ Meenach

Bridge, where the road intersects with Pettit Drive. A body's been found along the river at the base of Doomsday Hill."

Ivy recalled the sinister vulture peering down from the top of the hill and shuddered.

Chapter 15

Finding Danny Darkfoot

Sunday

Rex reached the body first. He smelled it before he saw it. The body emitted a putrid odor, almost a cross between rotting fruit and feces. The stench was familiar and immediately sent Rex into detective mode. He directed one of the people who had found the body to call 9-1-1 and ask that police and an ambulance be sent immediately. He knew there wouldn't be anything the Spokane Fire Department EMTs could do – just officially verify the death.

O'Dendren arrived and began securing the area. He commanded the two women and the man who had found the body to wait. They were too shocked, and at the same time, too curious to leave anyway. Other race spectators began to gather and two EMTs from their first aid station at the top of Doomsday Hill arrived to help after seeing the crowd collecting.

The body lay face down in the cheatgrass and knapweed along the riverbank. It appeared to be a young man, with short, black hair and bangs. Dirt and debris stuck to the disheveled hair, which was matted with dry blood. The man's dark clothing and orange vest were ripped, dirtied and bloodied. Horrifying and disturbing, the corpse did not have any hands. Ragged edges of skin remained where the hands should have been. Maggots crawled on the loose flaps of skin.

Rex was thankful he ate a light breakfast that morning. Until the rest of the homicide unit could arrive with equipment and photograph the scene, he wouldn't turn the body over. There was nothing the EMTs could do for whoever this had been. Instead, they assisted one of the bystanders who had gone into shock.

Fortunately, they didn't have to wait long. When Ivy and the rest of the homicide team arrived, she handed Rex a pair of sweats and a hoodie. "I pulled these off a tree near the starting line of the race," she explained. "Thought you might need some more clothes."

Ivy had rushed to the downtown police station after speaking with the officer by the finisher t-shirt tables. It was closer than her house and she kept a change of clothes there. She grabbed her homicide investigation kit, stuffed in extra gloves, and joined the rest of the team. They pushed through the crowds downtown and circumnavigated the race route to get to the crime scene.

"Thanks," said Rex, who had started to cool off now that he was no longer running. It wasn't Dolce and Gabbana, but it would have to do. The gray, baggy sweats looked like they came from a second-hand store. And they probably did.

He assigned Ivy to interview the people who found the body while he determined the perimeter of the crime scene, and another team member photographed the body and surrounding area. Now that backup had arrived, Sergeant O'Dendren joined Rex and the others searching for clues in a grid pattern along the grassy slope.

"I like your outfit," O'Dendren said, nodding at Rex. "A present from Ivy?"

"Yes, yours too?" Rex eyed the Sergeant's pale yellow sweatshirt with sleeves much too short in the arms.

Otherwise, they mostly worked in silence. While in the distance, the sound of thousands of feet running over pavement, bands playing, loudspeakers urging on racers and a helicopter flying overhead told them the race continued without them.

By the time the team finished examining and photographing the surrounding area and the body, a medical examiner had joined them. Due to the large number of people in town and the race activities, an additional medical examiner was on call for the weekend and was able to provide the main office with assistance. It was time to roll the body over and see the face.

"We won't be identifying this fellow by his fingerprints," O'Dendren stated the obvious as the medical examiner carefully rolled the body onto its back. Everyone steeled themselves for what they expected to see next.

"Oh no!" exclaimed Ivy, just returning from taking statements and contact information from the people who found the body. Even though decomposition had started and she didn't have Danny's photo with her, she recognized the young man's tattoos. A wallet with identification found in a pocket confirmed Ivy's suspicion.

"He's not just missing his hands," said the Medical Examiner, Betty Dyde. "The bullet wound in the back of his head was the likely cause of death. But someone also cut out his tongue."

"What about a bullet?" asked Rex. "Is it still in the body?"

"I don't see an exit wound. It might be lodged in the skull. The decomposition is bad. I'll get an entomologist to look at this blowfly larva. That'll give us an idea of how long this guy's been dead. I should be able to give you a complete report after a thorough examination. We've got to get this body out of the weeds and into an examining room, though."

"This looks like the work of a professional. It wasn't a robbery. He still had his wallet. The shot to the back of the head – looks like an execution," opined Rex. "And the hands and tongue were removed to send a message."

"What's the message?" asked Ivy.

"Don't talk."

"Sorry."

"No. I mean the killer is sending a message to someone warning them not to talk." Rex had recognized Danny Darkfoot also, and wondered if there might be a connection with the beating of Scout Blueblood. "The chief will be interested in this case."

"I need to get the body back to the morgue. Are we through here?" asked Dyde.

"I'll call Tribal Chief Andy Blueblood and ask him to bring the grandmother in to officially ID the body," said Rex, before releasing the medical examiner with the body.

The detective did a quick check. They had surveyed, photographed, taken measurements and sketched the scene and the body. Ivy had compiled the witnesses' statements. Fortunately, the media was focused on the race and were not aware yet of this ghastly development. The homicide squad had completed the search uninterrupted. Rex called Chief Barney Blueblood and Tribal Chief Andy Blueblood.

After updating both chiefs with the latest details about the situation, Rex turned to Ivy and said, "The chief's with the mayor. Prosciutto's been frantic since hearing about the discovery of the body. He's trying to keep news about the murder from overshadowing attention on the race and the winners."

"I wonder who won?" asked Ivy, meaning the race, but looking at O'Dendren and knowing he would be out $100. And they'd have to eat crow when they saw Chief Blaize.

Rex was thinking about how sad Danny's grandmother would be when she learned of her grandson's demise. It looked like the bear from her dream did snare Danny.

The senior detective and Sergeant O'Dendren caught a ride back to the station with Ivy. They missed the Bloomsday Race Corporate Cup Party and the medal ceremony. Fire Chief Blaize and The Heat would be celebrating and gloating. At least until they found out why Rex and O'Dendren didn't finish the race.

Chapter 16

POSTMORTEM

Monday Morning, Second Week of May

Early Monday, Rex stretched his sore leg muscles under his favorite table in Cafe Noir. The best aspect of having the race over was that he could now relax with a delicious cappuccino in the morning instead of getting sweaty and exhausted running before work.

He pulled out the *Spokane Lede* and read the front-page story about the race. As predicted, the Kenyan, Sokoro, won the men's division and Misha Middendorff, the Russian, won the women's division. A woman from Seattle was the highest placing American, coming in second in the women's division. The Eastern Washington University team barely edged out the The Heat in the corporate cup division. News of the body found along the route was on the second page. At the top of the page was a picture of the costumed vulture on Doomsday Hill. Rex was sure the mayor would not like the optics of the vulture picture on the same page as the murder story.

"Hey Rex, where's your Bloomsday t-shirt?" asked Gina. Wearing a finisher t-shirt the following day was another of the many Bloomsday traditions. She set down his drink with the usual foam heart on top. The heart warmed Rex almost as much as the coffee did.

"No t-shirt this year. I got waylaid on a case. Had to work and wasn't able to finish the race."

"Oh Rex. I'm so sorry. I know how much you wanted to compete this year," she sympathized.

He almost wished it were true. "Maybe next year."

Few other customers frequented the cafe this early. Except for the hissing of the espresso machine and Gina's friendly banter, the quiet of the cafe afforded Rex the perfect environment for dissecting a homicide case.

The search of the crime scene the day before yielded no evidence to indicate the murder took place at the location where the body was found by the river. In fact, the evidence showed just the opposite. The mangled vegetation and marks in the dirt indicated the body was dumped and rolled down the gentle slope. It also appeared that even though Danny Darkfoot had been dead for a few days at least, the body was deposited recently.

Maybe the lab results would give a clue as to where the murder took place.

Rex pondered thoughtfully over his coffee. The Bloomsday race volunteers would have traveled the entire route before the race as they shut the streets and checked the route for hazards. He needed to find out when they last checked the route before the race. And could they have missed the body if it were there already? Possibly, if they traveled the route and shut the streets before sunrise.

Was the killer sending a message? If so, to whom? And what was the message? To be quiet? About what?

Rex mulled over what he knew about Danny Darkfoot. Danny's parents had split up when he was young and the boy had a troubled upbringing. The only family he possessed in the area was his grandmother. Danny had served time for selling drugs in the past. Was his murder somehow connected? If he was only freelance guiding, was he also selling drugs to make a living? A bullet to the back of the head was a common way for drug dealers to rid themselves of a rival, or one of their own if a deal went bad, or a person who knew too much or turned to assist police.

Rex also knew that Danny worked, at least occasionally, for Varmint Outfitters. He was a guide on a hunt in which one of the clients accidentally shot himself. Supposedly. Had someone else killed the client and Danny knew about it? Or, had Danny killed the client and Danny's death was revenge? If so, why would Boone Crockett and the other guides lie?

And was there a connection between Danny's death and his friend Scout Blueblood? Chief Blueblood and his brother both claimed Danny and Scout had been hanging out together the past few months. Danny worked for Varmint Outfitters and Scout was employed just down the street at Tom's Taxidermy. Would the medical examiner's report show that Danny died before, or after, Scout was beaten?

Rex and Ivy planned to review the case with Chief Blueblood and Tribal Chief Andy Blueblood after the departmental, Monday morning briefing. He should give Sheriff Wyatt a courtesy call, too. They would have the medical examiner's report that afternoon but other evidence, such as soil and blood samples, could be at the lab for a few days.

Rex devised more questions than answers at this point. It sure would help if Scout Blueblood came out of his coma. According to Danny's grandmother, Scout was Danny's only real friend. And Danny's employer Boone Crockett didn't even acknowledge knowing him. Maybe Crockett would be more cooperative now that the crime being investigated was murder.

Customers started trickling into Cafe Noir. Soon the place would fill up. Time for Rex to leave. Chief Blueblood's Monday morning briefing would be starting soon.

"Morning, Boss," said Ivy, as she watered the veritable jungle around her desk, when Rex entered the office. She wore her Bloomsday finisher t-shirt beneath her blazer. "Molly Murrow called. She wants to talk to you about the body found during the race yesterday."

"She does?" Molly Murrow, a reporter with KRUM-TV, possessed a nose for news. A rather cute nose, thought Rex. He and Molly had a history but when she left Spokane for the bigger stations in Seattle after college, Rex let her go. He just wasn't sure about disrupting his quiet lifestyle, especially with an investigative reporter. Since then, Molly had married, divorced and returned to Spokane. Rex remained single, mostly content with his solitary, introverted lifestyle. But Molly's presence made him feel like something was missing in his solitude.

"Nice t-shirt," said Rex as he took the phone message from Ivy. "At least you have something to show for all that training we did."

"Yeah, I feel sorry that you and Phil weren't able to finish the race."

"I don't know what's worse — not getting a t-shirt, or seeing the smug grin on Chief Blaize when I pay him a hundred bucks," lamented Sergeant O'Dendren, walking into the room with a large cup of coffee and a jelly donut.

"Or spending a day washing..." Ivy began playfully.

"Let's get started," Chief Blueblood called over his shoulder as he headed for the hallway.

Rex regretted being involved in this stupid bet. He gave Ivy a withering look as they joined the other officers funneling into the conference room where the chief would hand out new assignments for the week and they would discuss any pertinent information that needed to be exchanged.

When the chief addressed the Darkfoot murder, he explained, "The mayor wants this case buried. He wants it solved quickly and with minimal media coverage. Bloomsday is an economic boon to the city. He doesn't want a murder case staining the event. He's still hosting international visitors and wants them to see only the best the Lilac City has to offer.

"Lastly, O'Dendren, Hemlock, Pine, Begonia and Lizei, we'll be washing fire trucks at Station One the last weekend this month."

"Ahh Chief, no fair. Rex and Phil didn't get to finish the race. Our team didn't have a chance," complained Hollywood.

"Life's not fair. But we honor our word here in this department. The last thing I need is Chief Blaize on my back, accusing us of not keeping our promises."

Not fair? Washing fire trucks? He hadn't been part of any bet, thought Rex. And yet, somehow he was included in the truck washing.

After the briefing, Rex and Ivy joined Tribal Chief Andy Blueblood, who had just arrived, and their own chief in his office.

"I've just come from the morgue," said Andy. "I took Winnie Milne in to ID the body. It was Danny alright. His grandmother was really shaken up. Danny spoke to her in a dream. She dreamed that he told her a bear had killed him. She's spending the day with a niece here in town. I'll pick her up and take her back to the reservation later."

"Did she say whether she saw or heard from Danny since we talked with her three weeks ago?" asked Rex.

"Only in the dream. Danny Darkfoot hasn't been seen on the reservation since just before the incident with Scout."

Rex updated them on what details were known about the Darkfoot case. "We're expecting the autopsy report this morning," he added. "Lab results from the soil and blood samples might take another day."

"Any news on Scout? It would sure help if we could talk with him."

"I'm stopping by the hospital after leaving here. I'll let you know if anything has changed," said Andy.

He looked so sad. Ivy, who enjoyed a close relationship with her own father, sympathized with the tribal police chief.

Rex and Ivy returned to their desks. The autopsy report had arrived. As suspected, the gunshot wound to the back of the head was listed as the cause of death. The medical examiner had removed a bullet lodged in the skull. It was from a 9 mm Glock. The hands and tongue were removed after Danny was shot. Decomposition made facial recognition difficult, but the distinctive tattoos of the Salish writing on the neck and the mountains and coyote on the arms suggested the body was his. Dental records and a DNA test confirmed it.

Internally, the body contained traces of heroin. Externally, the medical examiner had found tiny pieces of grass, pine bark, pine needles and soil not associated with the site where the body was discovered. It appeared the body had been wrapped in a blue tarp from the tiny, plastic fibers found clinging to the clothing. Danny had been dead for about two weeks.

His body hadn't been lying at the base of Doomsday Hill all that time. Ivy called the Bloomsday Race organizers. They explained that volunteers had set up road barricades along the race route the evening before the race. They drove the route again just before the start of the race to ensure no one had placed obstacles along the route. Barricades blocked the road just above the slope where the body was discovered. The race director told Ivy that the volunteers hadn't seen the body or anything out of the ordinary in the area it was discovered. He gave her the names and contact information of the volunteers so she could follow-up with them. A water station and first aid station were positioned at the top of the hill. Did anyone there notice anything unusual? The race director didn't know but would get the names of everyone working in the area that morning and pass along Ivy's inquiry and contact information. Wait, there was a band set up near the bottom of the hill. He would get her the band leader's information too.

Rex stood up, stretched, and then strode into the break room to make a cappuccino. He needed a shot of strong espresso to wake his tired brain – a brain fixated on the Darkfoot case. Danny was a young Indian man who didn't have much going for him in life. Could Rex make sense of his death?

Danny had been missing for over a week before he died and then his body went undetected for a week. Finally, his body showed up along the route of one of Spokane's largest events with thousands of race participants, volunteers, and spectators. It was as if the killer wanted to make sure the body was found. The racers wouldn't necessarily see the body. They would be focused on the race. But there were sure to be enough people in the vicinity that the body would be discovered. Was there a connection to the race? And if so, why that specific spot? Was it as simple as the location was easy to reach undetected? Or was there a significance to the base of Doomsday Hill with the vulture lurking at the top?

Cappuccino in hand, Rex returned to his desk and began reading Ivy's notes taken while interviewing the spectators who found the body. They were students at Spokane Falls Community College and had walked along the route to the crest of Doomsday Hill that morning to watch as the first racers topped the hill. After the elite racers passed, they had headed back toward the school where they planned to do lab work during the afternoon. At the bottom of the hill, one of them had noticed something bright orange in the weeds and they all had smelled an awful odor. As the students approached the orange object, they saw a hunting vest. But it was the handless body wearing the vest that had caused them to scream and the putrid stench that had caused them to vomit. They hadn't noticed anyone else down by the river or along the slope.

On her computer, Ivy enlarged a section of the Bloomsday Race map between miles three and five, laid it over an enlarged street map and topographic map and printed the compilation. She and Rex marked the location of the body and the known volunteer stations and bands along the route. The roads south and east of the crime scene were part of the closed off race route. The road north of the scene led to residential areas. To the west, Downriver Drive skirted a golf course before heading toward Riverside State Park. There weren't any nearby businesses with security cameras.

It was closing in on noon and Rex began thinking about another part of town. "How would you like to go back to Tofucious for lunch today?" he asked Ivy. "I'd like to ask Boone Crockett a few more questions."

The phone rang. It was Molly Murrow.

Chapter 17

LUNCH IN HILLYARD

Monday Afternoon

Molly met the two detectives at Tofucious in the Hillyard neighborhood. "Thanks for letting me crash your lunch date," she teased Rex when they were all sitting at a table in the back of the restaurant.

Ivy perked up and looked quizzically over the top of her menu at the senior detective, who blushed and quickly ducked behind his menu without explanation. Glancing over at Molly, Ivy caught her wink.

Molly ordered the bibimbap special while Rex and Ivy each chose the kimchi noodles.

"I'm hoping you can tell me more about the body found along the Bloomsday Race route," Molly continued. "What's the story? Rumors are floating that the mayor's political opponents are trying to embarrass him while the spotlight is on the city for the race, and that they hired a mob hit to shine a light where the mayor doesn't want any light shining."

Who comes up with these rumors, Rex wondered. "So far, it's a story with few details," he answered. "The body was identified as Danny Darkfoot, a young man who went missing off the Spokane Reservation a couple of weeks ago. We don't know how he ended up along the race route. It could be entirely unrelated to the race."

"What about the gunshots to the back of the head and the missing hands and tongue. Don't tell me those are just rumors? Isn't that characteristic of a mob killing?"

He knew Molly, as an investigative reporter, asked hard questions in order to dispel any rumors and get to the truth, but he wished she would refrain from the mob references. Mayor Sammy Prosciutto was proud of his

Italian heritage and more than a little sensitive to the stereotype of Italian mafia, especially as it related to his politics. Having Italian heritage himself, Rex could sympathize. At least a little. "It just means the killer had a gun and access to a sharp blade," he said.

"We do know now that Danny Darkfoot was not killed at the location where his body was found. There were thousands of people in the area Sunday morning. It could help if KRUM-TV put out a request for information from anyone who may have seen anything unusual that morning." Although Rex resented a reporter's inquisitiveness, Molly had helped solve cases in the past and he was grateful for her assistance.

"Done. We'll do that Detective Begonia, but I do want to be the first to hear when you apprehend the murderer," Molly said, and winked.

Ivy looked around the room. She noticed Tom Cathartes enter the restaurant, slip behind the counter, and then walk into the kitchen. Curious, she excused herself and quietly moved toward the door to the kitchen. She remembered seeing him the last time she ate here and hoped there wasn't a connection between the restaurant and the taxidermy shop. The thought made her feel queasy. Standing on her toes, she could see through the door's window and into the kitchen. Tom was flailing his arms and shouting at someone out of Ivy's view. Tom looked upset. She couldn't hear what was being said but could tell it was a heated discussion.

"What was that all about?" Rex asked Ivy when she returned to the table. "I'm not sure. I saw the taxidermist, Tom Cathartes, go into the kitchen. He was here last time we ate here, too. We might want to stick with the vegetarian options next time."

After finishing lunch, Molly hurried off to another story – the mayor was hosting a Sister City event in Manito Park – and the two detectives walked toward Varmint Outfitters. As they neared the business, a young man exited and climbed into the cab of a large, black pickup with the name 'Kam's Landscaping' on the side.

"I've never heard of Kam's Landscaping," noted Ivy, whose family owned Lizei Nursery, famous in the Northwest for high-quality plants and landscape designs. In turn, Ivy's family knew almost every landscaping company in the county and surrounding areas. "But that guy looks familiar. Like I've seen him recently."

As they opened the door to Varmint Outfitters, she looked back and noticed the pickup drive down the street and park in front of Tom's Taxidermy Shop.

Once inside, the two detectives waited while the petite blonde fetched Boone Crockett. It was Ivy's turn to scrutinize the trophy hunter photos on the walls. Even just one plant would improve the decor in here, she thought decidedly.

"Detective Begonia. Looks like you brought backup. Did you find your hunter?" bellowed Crockett as he emerged from his office. With a disdainful glance, he dismissed Rex's diminutive partner.

Rex noticed that the outfitter didn't offer them chairs, or more importantly, coffee.

"You may have seen the news. Danny Darkfoot's body was found near TJ Meenach Bridge yesterday during the Bloomsday Race."

"I did see that."

"When was the last time Darkfoot guided for you?" asked Rex.

"Like I said before, he wasn't a regular employee. Just helped out when we needed an extra guide."

"And when would that have been?" the detective pressed.

"I can't recall. Weeks ago. Months maybe."

"Surely you keep records," Rex was beginning to feel impatient. "After all, a squeaky-clean operation has to have employment records for tax purposes," he added, poignantly.

"All right, take a seat in my office," growled Crockett. He pulled a file from a cabinet, scanned the contents and then followed the detectives into his office. He sat down behind a large oak desk while Rex and Ivy took seats across the vast surface from him.

"The last hunt Darkfoot guided was four weeks ago. A black bear foray up in the Selkirks."

"Isn't this an unusual time of year to hunt bear? Haven't they been hibernating?" asked Ivy. Beau had told her that spring hunts originated as a way to control bear damage to trees. Still, she wanted to hear Crockett's explanation.

"Most hunting is done in the fall but we also have a spring bear hunt until mid-June in Washington. Special permit areas. Just can't shoot the sows and cubs. Need to keep the population going so we can have another hunt next year."

"Did you see Darkfoot after the hunt?" asked Rex.

"Of course. I was on the hunt. Me and a couple of the guides and some high-paying clients. We bagged two bears. Once we got back in town, he took his pay and left. Last I saw of Danny."

"Did you notice anything out of the ordinary? How did he get along with the other guides and the clients?"

"Nothing unusual. A bit of scrapping with a couple of the other guides, but that happens. The guys can get competitive, and Danny got mouthy sometimes. Didn't know when to shut up. But he was a damn good tracker." Crockett actually sounded a little sad.

"How about drugs or alcohol?" Rex pursued. It sounded like Crockett knew Danny better than he initially indicated.

"You don't hunt much do you, Detective?" Crockett snarled. "None of my boys touch a drop when they're hunting with clients, but they can cut loose in camp. Our clients hunt to bring home trophy animals but they're out in the woods to have a good time too."

"Did Danny bring any drugs?"

"Maybe he did. Maybe he didn't. Wasn't a problem."

Ivy raised an eyebrow.

"What can you tell us about a hunt last fall, the one in which a client died? Was Danny guiding on that hunt, too?"

"Look. I told the sheriff all about that. Varmint Outfitters was cleared. It was a hunting accident."

"I just want to know if Danny was there," Rex pressed.

Crockett glowered. "Are you arresting me? If not, then I don't have anything more to say to you."

If he could, Rex would have arrested Crockett for rudeness but since that wasn't an option and they didn't have any evidence that tied Crockett to Danny's murder, he would have to try another approach. More than one way to skin a cat, or bear, thought Rex as they left the building.

In the car as they drove back to the station, Ivy pointed out, "Didn't it seem odd that he referenced a file to tell us that Danny Darkfoot worked for him four weeks ago?"

Chapter 18

A BREAK

Wednesday, Third Week in May

By the following midweek, Rex and Ivy had made slow progress on the Darkfoot case, but still hadn't learned anything new regarding Scout Blueblood. They spent three days on the reservation interviewing everyone who knew Scout. No new information came forth from their efforts. Rex made follow-up calls to Louie at the casino and to Sheriff Wyatt, but there wasn't any additional information on those fronts either. If the Darkfoot and Blueblood cases were connected, solving one might solve the other, Rex knew.

He stood contemplating the map on the wall in the office – the map showing the race route and location where Danny's body was found. The aroma of caffeine wafted upwards from the Italian ceramic cup he held. He sighed heavily.

Earlier in the week, Rex had received the lab reports confirming soil and other debris found on Danny Darkfoot's body came from a location other than where the body was found. Small pieces of bluegrass, bentgrass, cheatgrass, arborvitae, knapweed, pine needles and bark clung to Darkfoot's clothing. Only some of these plants could be found at the site. The others were more common to a residential yard. The lab technicians had identified clay and loam particles soiling the clothing in addition to the sandy loam from along the riverbank. The entomologist had determined Danny was dead for two weeks by the time the body was found.

After Molly Murrow's report on KRUM-TV, witnesses came forward to report seeing a dark gray van with a white stripe in the area of TJ Meenach Bridge the morning of the race. An all points bulletin was issued for the van, which sported a Stop Keystone bumper sticker on the back window. Also,

Ivy discovered two members of the Siberian Slayers, a heavy metal band stationed at the base of Doomsday Hill, had criminal records for assault, hate crimes and poaching. Coincidence? Rex and Ivy would visit them later this morning.

"Hey, Boss, we've got a break!" shouted Ivy, while setting the receiver down on her office phone. "That was the sheriff's office. A park ranger at Riverside State Park reported an abandoned van found in the brush. It's a 1985 Chevy, dark gray with a white stripe on the side and a Stop Keystone sticker on back. Some geocaching hikers found the van hidden in the brush. They called it in because it looked abandoned."

"Sheriff Wyatt thought we might like to look around before she has the vehicle hauled out of the woods. The license plate is missing, but it does match the description of Danny Darkfoot's van."

"Sounds like our itinerary today just changed," said Rex, hopeful that progress would finally be made on the case. The heavy metal band would have to wait.

The sheriff's team would already be examining the van and surrounding area, but the two detectives grabbed their crime scene kits anyway. With the abandoned van found in the county and the body discovered in the city, they faced a multi-jurisdictional crime. And where did the murder take place, Rex wondered as he and Ivy climbed into their vehicle. He couldn't rule out the reservation or casino, which meant tribal jurisdiction. Either way, he needed to let Chief Andy Blueblood know Danny was found.

Riverside State Park lay nine miles northwest of the downtown core. Downriver Drive followed the Spokane River as it wound toward the park from TJ Meenach Bridge. Other routes to the park existed but Rex and Ivy chose this road to gain a sense of where the van may have driven. As they passed the bridge heading west, the narrow road squeezed between the river on the left and a golf course on the right. A few cars were parked in the scattering of pullouts where cyclists and hikers could disperse onto trails in the 1400-acre park spanning both sides of the river. They passed the wastewater plant and the entrance to a campground. Rex wondered why anyone would choose to camp near a wastewater treatment plant before making a note to check the plant's surveillance cameras.

Finally, they turned off the main road when they saw a parked deputy's car.

Ninebark and snowberry bushes hid the entrance to a gravel road leading into the woods. The sheriff's team had cordoned off the area around the van and taken photographs.

"Good afternoon, detectives. Looks like we have a vehicle you might be interested in," said a sheriff's deputy as Rex and Ivy approached. "Got a search warrant for it this morning."

"Afternoon. What have you found, so far?" asked Rex, ignoring the deputy's resemblance to a car salesman pitching a new model. The van matched the description of Danny's vehicle. Was this where he met his demise? Or was the van dumped here after transporting his body?

"Just the van. Some fast-food wrappers and cups, an old jacket in the back, sunglasses, pens, some weed and a bag with heroin residue in the glove compartment. No vehicle title or anything showing ownership. Even the license plate's been stripped."

"How about the surrounding area? Bullet casings or anything indicating a murder took place here?" Rex asked.

"Nothing in the surrounding area. Except if you look closely, there's some dried blood on the back bumper. It looks like someone tried to clean off the blood but missed a spot. Whoever it was must have known we would eventually identify the van, but it looks like they tried to cover their tracks to slow us down. When you're done looking around, we'll have the van taken into the State Patrol's local crime lab and have it processed for fingerprints and DNA. Also, we'll get that blood on the bumper analyzed."

"Thanks, Officer...?"

"Rygg. Deputy Otto Rygg. I'll have a copy of the lab report sent to your office, Detective."

Although the sheriff's team collected evidence, the two detectives also took photographs of the van and the surrounding wooded area. The van left distinctive tire tracks. Rex recalled the rain the night before the race. It looked like the van may have been driven into the woods either during or shortly after the rain. When the detectives finished, they checked back in with Deputy Rygg and then headed toward the office.

"Do we have time to make a quick stop at Lizei Nursery?" Ivy asked. "It's not far out of the way and I need to pick up some bonsai tools from my dad. Now that the race is over, I need to spend more time in the garden."

Rex was happy to oblige. He could easily spend hours browsing the plants, examining the new varieties, smelling fragrant flowers and absorbing the ambiance. He sighed. They'd have to keep the visit short this time. As they pulled up in front of the nursery, a man jumped into a black pickup towing a trailer piled with small shrubs and drew away from the curb. Kam's Landscaping was printed on the side.

"Hey, I've seen that pickup recently," said Ivy. "It was parked outside Varmint Outfitters the last time we visited. I thought I recognized the guy getting into the pickup that day, but I couldn't quite place him."

"I remember," acknowledged Rex. "Must have been working on a job in Hillyard."

They found Joe Lizei, Ivy's father, dividing yellow water lilies in the nursery's section devoted to wetland plants and water features.

"Hi, Pop. We stopped by for the jin pliers and shari knife," said Ivy, reaching out to give her father a big hug. She didn't think twice about hugging him while on duty or in front of her colleague.

With a beaming smile on his face, Joe returned Ivy's hug before pulling off his garden gloves and extending a hand to Rex. "Nice to see you again, Detective."

"Good to see you too, Joe. How's business?" Rex asked.

"Oh, business is growing, as usual," Joe grinned happily. "It's spring and everyone in Spokane starts craving greenery and blossoms after hibernating all winter," he explained. It was true. The Lilac City boasted a plethora of garden clubs and events. Every year, thousands of citizens flocked to nurseries to buy hanging baskets of flowers, tomato starts, and more, anxious to get the gardening season started. This year, a hard winter with record snowfall prompted a veritable plant frenzy among the populace once spring hit.

Joe went to get the pliers and knife. When he returned and handed them to Ivy, she asked, "Did you know the guy that left the nursery as we arrived? He was short and kinda muscular. Had dark hair and beard. He was wearing jeans and a gray hoodie."

"Alex Kamchatka? Alex was here just before you showed up. Why?" her father asked.

"Kamchatka? That's it – Kam's Landscaping!" Ivy realized excitedly. "I thought I knew all of the landscapers in town, but apparently not. What do you know about him?"

"Well, Alex is the owner of Kam's Landscaping. He's been doing business here for a little over a year. His family emigrated from Russia shortly before that. He started the landscaping business and hired other young immigrants from the former Soviet Union countries. Like many new immigrants, they stick together. They've done some high-end landscaping jobs, like a contract with Wes Larch's golf courses. I don't know anything more than that. I only know him professionally. What's your interest in Alex?" Joe asked.

"I've seen his truck around town. Last week, I saw him leaving Varmint Outfitters."

"Kamtchatka? Hey, he might be one of the guides working for Varmint Outfitters. He probably thinks we're following him," suggested Rex, as he pulled out the hunting brochure from his jacket pocket.

"So, he's Russian," said Ivy, thinking aloud. "He looks familiar, but I'm not sure where I would have met him."

"He's not the only immigrant from there working in the business. After the breakup of the Soviet Union, a number of Russians, Ukrainians and others came to America. A large contingent settled here in Spokane," Joe explained. "Now a new generation has followed. Many started or joined yard care businesses. A few with excellent English skills and more ambition, like Alex, started their own landscaping businesses. They're cutthroat competitive."

Ivy made a note in her phone's memo app. "Thanks for the info. We've got to get going, Pop, but I'll stop by for dinner later. I'm bringing a friend. See you then."

"We've got time for one more stop on the way back to the station," Rex told Ivy as they slid into their Crown Victoria. "Let's see if Bruno Hentan is home. I'd like to know more about Siberian Slayers' activities the day Danny Darkfoot was murdered."

Late afternoon shadows stretched across the ground as the detectives pulled onto a brush-lined driveway that led about a half-block from the road on the far west edge of the city. Wild rose bushes, spirea and ninebark obscured the house from view. Rusted relics of vehicles lay littered throughout the weedy yard. At the end of the driveway and next to a ramshackle house, sat a blue 1978 GMC pickup with its hood lifted. Rex and Ivy caught a glimpse of two men behind the hood. Heavy metal music thumping from speakers in the house drowned out the crunch of tires on gravel as the detectives approached.

When they got out of the Crown Vic, a skunky smell hit Ivy's nose. Was it an animal or pot? Either seemed likely. It permeated the air. The sun disappeared behind a dark cloud and a sudden coolness raised the hair on the back of her neck. Ivy's body tensed with alertness.

A large man holding a ratchet wrench stepped from behind the hood of the pickup. A tiger tattoo decorated his bald head just above his right ear. Tattoos covered his neck and his sleeveless arms all the way to his grease-soiled hands. A bushy mustache couldn't hide the frown on his ruddy face.

The second, shorter man, walked around from the other side of the pickup. His stringy, dirty-blond hair hung down past his shoulders to his black t-shirt with a picture of a saber-toothed tiger on it and the words Siberian Slayer. Around his neck, he wore a bear claw pendent hanging from a leather cord. He, too, held a wrench.

They must be Bruno Hentan, the bassist, and Russ Lear, the drummer, thought Ivy as she recalled reviewing their criminal records. Did they think a saber-toothed tiger was a Siberian tiger, she ruminated.

"Who are you?" growled the taller man, eyeing the detectives in their jackets and slacks. "You look like cops."

"Detectives Begonia and Lizei," said Rex, holding up his badge. "We just have a few questions to ask you."

"I don't talk to cops," the large man answered. The shorter one remained quiet and watched the exchange.

"You do if you want to remain on the outside, breathing this fresh air," said Rex. "We know your record and we know you were in the vicinity of the body found along the race route on Bloomsday. We can take you in for questioning, or we can have a friendly conversation right here."

"We don't know nothing about no body. We had a gig to play. Why would we stick around if we plugged some dude? You think we're stupid or something?"

Rex wasn't going to answer that. "How did you know Danny Darkfoot?" he asked, hoping that if they did, they'd be tricked into responding.

"Danny was a dealer. We didn't have nuthin to do with him."

"You were in prison together," said Ivy, staring down the large man.

He glowered back. "Yeah, so? Don't mean we hung out together. I seen him around town after I got out, but I don't hang with his kind."

"Tell us about the morning of the race. What did you do?"

"We set up. We had to be there and set up by 8:00. So we didn't have time to do nothing else."

"Did anyone see you?"

"Yeah. The other guys in the band. Also, the race officials came by to make sure we was set up."

"Did you see anything unusual? Anyone down by the river? Or a gray van?"

"I don't know. It's been awhile since the gig. I don't hardly remember yesterday," he sneered.

"How about you?" Rex asked, directing his attention to the smaller man.

"He don't talk to cops either," said the larger man.

"Well let's just hope we don't have any more questions for you then," said Rex as the detectives turned to go. They needed more than proximity to the body on race day to tie these two to the Darkfoot case.

"One more question," said Ivy, reeling around before getting in the car. "What's a Siberian Slayer? Is that someone who slays Siberians, or is it a Siberian who slays?"

"Huh?" the two men asked in unison.

Chapter 19

CONNECTING THE EVIDENCE

Tuesday, Fourth Week of May

In a reluctant recognition that he needed to do more to stay in shape, Rex had agreed to run with Ivy before work Tuesday morning. At least daylight hours continued to lengthen in May. In a few months, Rex might not be as willing to be so active before his morning cappuccino. He waited for her by the clock tower in the park. They planned to run along the flat Centennial Trail. No more killer hills.

Ivy bubbled with excitement when she arrived. "Boss, you'll never guess," she said as they jogged eastward alongside the river, where lilac bushes along the banks filled the air with a light, floral scent. "So, I'll just tell you. We're not the only ones interested in Varmint Outfitters or Tom's Taxidermy. Last night at dinner, Beau told me about a smuggling investigation the Department of Fish and Wildlife has been conducting for the past year. I think it could have a bearing on our case."

"Oh. How's that?" Rex gasped from the exertion.

"Remember during the carbo-loading dinner before Bloomsday, Beau told us how that case with the bear carcass involved poaching? Well, the Fish and Wildlife Department's been investigating illegal bear hunting and smuggling and have been watching Varmint Outfitters and Tom's Taxidermy for over a year. Beau knows Boone Crockett and Tom Cathartes. He even knows about Alex Kamtchatka and Hentan and Lear. Would you believe their records include poaching?"

"Interesting. Do you think your Beau would like to meet us for lunch today?" asked Rex. "Let's say noon at the Asian Fusion. Maybe he could give us some background information on these bear bandits."

"Sure. I think he's in the office and not out in the field today. I'll check."

Later that morning at the station while reviewing a report showing the weapons registered to Boone Crockett, Rex received a call from the regional crime lab. The forensics investigation of the van found at Riverside State Park was finished. Earlier, Deputy Rygg had reported that the vehicle identification number on the van matched that of Danny Darkfoot's vehicle. The forensics report now showed the blood DNA on the bumper matched Danny's DNA. Rex told Crys Beaker, crime lab supervisor, that he and Ivy would stop by to pick up and discuss the report before lunch.

As they were preparing to leave the station, Fire Chief Billy Blaize jauntily sauntered past on his way to visit Chief Blueblood. "Hey detectives. We'll see you on Saturday," he called out.

Rex forgot Saturday was wash day. The task was rescheduled once already. Now he had to block out a second weekend. "I'm still not happy about being volunteered for washing fire trucks," he grumbled to Ivy as they walked by a chagrined Sergeant O'Dendren, who lowered his head.

"Let me bag up this soil sample and I'll be with you in a minute," said Beaker when Rex and Ivy arrived at the crime lab a short while later. "I've been fingerprinting soil this morning. In the past, forensics scientists just compared the chemical and physical structure of soils. But now, advances in soil microbiology are proving invaluable for establishing evidence. Next generation sequencing produces vast amounts of data that allow us to link specific soils to a suspect, victim or crime scene."

"Are they like human fingerprints?" asked Ivy.

"Not exactly. It's called fingerprinting because it's based on uniqueness, but it's more like genetics. The soil is full of micro-organisms. Just like your DNA can tell me that you are related to other people named Lizei or Begonia, next-generation sequencing of soil micro-organisms in a sample can tell me if they are related to micro-organisms found in, say, a specific Palouse farm field."

"Did you sequence soil from the van?" Ivy asked, not sure she fully understood what was meant by sequencing but grasped the importance of it for establishing forensic evidence.

"I've analyzed and set aside soil found in and on the van so it's ready for fingerprint comparisons in case you have a need later," answered the forensics expert.

"You mean if we obtain soil from a potential murder site?" asked Rex.

"Exactly. Also, I compared the blood found on the van's bumper with Danny Darkfoot's blood," Beaker added. "It was his. I also found his fingerprints on the trash in the back of the van. The rest of the van was wiped clean of prints, inside and out."

"How about the steering wheel? You didn't find any prints there?" Rex asked as he glanced through the report.

"Nope. Whoever left the van in the woods was thorough. Looks like a professional, not your garden variety criminal," said the forensics expert. "But I did find tiny fibers and pieces of plant debris in the van and they matched those found on Darkfoot's clothing. Between that and the blood, it's safe to say he was in the van."

"Looks like the killer didn't act alone," said Rex. "We didn't find any evidence that the murder took place at the van site. And if you didn't find fingerprints on the steering wheel, someone wiped the prints after abandoning the vehicle. The killer probably used the van to transport the body, drove it to the park and dumped it in the woods after removing the license plate and wiping it down. That means someone else likely gave the killer a ride from the park and helped move the body. The question is who? And where did they go?" He handed the report to Ivy.

"Hey," said Ivy, looking at the signature on the report. "Your name is Crystal? Crystal Beaker?"

"Yes, but I prefer Crys. Can you imagine growing up with a name like Crystal Beaker? High school chemistry class was murder!"

Chapter 20

CONNECTING THE CASES

Tuesday Afternoon

After leaving the lab, Rex and Ivy drove to the Asian Fusion restaurant to meet Wildlife Officer Beau Hunter for lunch. Rex had an ulterior motive. His brother-in-law, Nobu was the chef. Nobu made the best spaghetti Bolognese in town, surpassing that of even Mama Begonia, though Rex would never admit it to his mother.

Now as the two detectives sat with the wildlife officer at a discreet table in a back corner of the restaurant, Rex inhaled the savory aromas emanating from his bowl of pasta. Resorting to his usual lunchtime tactic, he encouraged his companions to speak so he could concentrate on listening and enjoying his meal.

"Ivy tells me you've been investigating Boone Crockett and Tom Cathartes," the senior detective prompted the young officer.

"Yes, it's part of a larger effort to halt smuggling black bear parts," said Beau. "In the past few years as bears have become scarce in Asia, illegal hunting and trafficking of black bears has increased here in the Northwest. The demand for bear parts in Asia is high and bears there are near extinction."

"I remember you telling us about the gall bladders and bile," said Rex. "But black bear hunting is legal here, right?"

"It is. But bear hunting is supposed to be sport, not the commercialization of resources. We don't want our bear population to go extinct. While most Americans may not want to encounter a bear in the wild, we still value them as part of the ecosystem. Currently, the population in the Northwest can sustain bear hunting – a spring season in some areas as well as the normal fall season throughout the region. A hunter can get a tag for one bear. In some areas with high populations, two tags are allowed. But if hunters get greedy, we can decimate the bear population here, too.

"A hunter who finds a buyer willing to pay $5,000 to $8,000 for a gallbladder may be tempted to kill more than one bear. Wildlife officers have found multiple animals killed and tagged with legal bear tags belonging to someone who's never stepped in the woods. Also, selling bear parts is prohibited in Washington. Not in Idaho. It's illegal to transport a bear to Idaho, where commerce in parts is allowed. It happens all the time. So, we have a real challenge here along the border," admitted Beau. "Bears killed in Washington often end up with Idaho tags."

"Is that where Crockett and Cathartes come in? Have they been illegally hunting and trafficking bear parts?" Rex asked.

"We've been watching them for awhile now. We hope to have enough evidence for convictions soon," Beau said. "There's a connection between Varmint Outfitters and Tom's Taxidermy, but we haven't figure it out yet.

"About three years ago, wildlife officers started finding bear carcasses with the gallbladders and paws removed. We arrested a few individuals, including a couple of Crockett's guides. Most of them just got a slap on the wrist. Many judges don't take wildlife law violations seriously."

Beau continued, "We started piecing cases together. It looked like Tom's Taxidermy and the Korean market were the common link. But then last fall, something happened. There's been a disruption. We haven't been able to prove anything yet, but we suspect a new player has bullied his way in and is trying to take over the bear market in this area."

Rex envisioned a battle between bulls and bears on Hillyard's Market Street. "What makes you think there's been a disruption?" he asked.

"We started hearing grumbling from a few of the redneck poachers we picked up. They aren't the brightest bunch. We can usually find one or two who will rat each other out. They complained they were being paid less money for bears," said Beau. "They fingered Tom. Said he told them his sources were paying less. About the same time, Cathartes started acting strangely, skittish. At first, we thought he might have discovered we were watching him. So, we pulled back for awhile.

"We also noticed the Korean Market store stopped selling bear meat last fall. Undercover agents, including myself, started frequenting the restaurant when it opened. We suspected the market and restaurant owner was the pipeline for trafficking the bear parts to Korea."

"So how does all of this relate to Danny Darkfoot? Or for that matter, Scout Blueblood?" Rex asked, reflecting on how they still weren't any closer to solving the original case.

"We know Danny worked for Varmint Outfitters and Scout worked for Tom's Taxidermy," Ivy offered. "Boone Crockett knew Scout and he also knew Tom Cathartes. Crockett recommended the taxidermist hire Scout. Scout and Danny were close friends who were spending a lot of time together and they both liked hunting. Is it just coincidence that something terrible happened to both men about the same time?"

"Were Danny or Scout ever arrested for illegal hunting or trafficking bear?" Rex asked the wildlife officer.

"No. We knew Danny served time for illegally selling drugs, but neither of the men had any run-ins with wildlife law enforcement. Of course, state hunting laws didn't apply to them on the reservation."

"Is it possible that either of them knew about the trafficking?" the senior detective asked.

"Possible," admitted Beau. "And just because they didn't have any previous poaching arrests, doesn't mean they weren't involved in any illegal hunting and trafficking operations their employers might have been conducting and we just didn't know it."

With Danny Darkfoot dead and Scout Blueblood in a coma, Rex wondered how they could find a definitive answer to the question. By now, the detectives and the wildlife officer had finished their meals and he could use an after-lunch caffeine boost.

Rex and Beau ordered coffee while Ivy opted for green tea. The waiter brought a plate of fortune cookies with their beverages. Since Rex knew Chef Nobu to be of Japanese descent, he couldn't quite understand the fortune cookies, but accepted the explanation that customers clamored for them.

Rex slowly sipped the dark elixir. The coffee sent a bouquet of nuttiness and chocolate to his one distinguishing feature – a prominent Roman nose. Like the drink itself, the Darkfoot case was complex. But maybe if he complicated it further by helping the young wildlife officer solve the bear trafficking case, he and Ivy, in return, would find answers to what happened to Danny and Scout.

"Maybe we can help each other," proposed Rex. "If you have enough evidence to indicate trafficking is occurring, we might be able to obtain warrants to look at financial and other business records. That could give you the evidence you need to make arrests."

"Financial records could help considerably," admitted Beau. "What can we do to help you?"

"Any chance that one or two of those bear poachers might be convinced to talk about Danny Darkfoot and Scout Blueblood?"

"I'll see about hunting down a loose-lipped poacher or two," Beau agreed.

"This looks like it might be for you," Rex said as he handed Ivy a fortune pulled from a cookie. The slip of paper read – 'Romance will take a wild turn.'

Chapter 21

STREAM OF CONSCIOUSNESS

Sunday, Last Week in May

Rex had just left the Holy Heart Hospital where he visited with the two chiefs, Andy Blueblood and his brother, Barney Blueblood, who were checking up on Scout. That meant arriving at Cafe Noir just as the throng of Sunday churchgoers exited St. Ignatius across the street. He hustled to secure his favorite seat by the window before the cafe filled with parishioners willing to be tempted by dark, delicious coffee, and sweet pastries.

After ordering the Vatican, an espresso with Frangelico, Rex settled into a reading trance with *Ulysses*. He didn't notice the hubbub of humanity all around him until he closed the cover on the last chapter. He had drained his cup an hour ago and barely noticed as Gina periodically refilled it with the best, regular coffee in town. He marveled at Joyce's revolutionary technique of using a stream of consciousness and a unique story structure – the entire story took place on a single day, June 16, 1904. He looked up just as Ivy entered the cafe.

Ivy scanned the crowded room. Sunlight poured in through the large windows, reflected off the pastry display cases and added to the brightness of the bold-colored light fixtures and mosaic tabletops. Sweet scents of fruit-filled pastries intermingled with a buttery whiff of croissant and the ever-present smell of coffee. Ivy spied Rex by the window and walked over to join him.

"Hi, Boss. Thought I might find you here," she said, by way of greeting.

"Good morning. Or... Is it afternoon?" Rex replied, quickly glancing at his watch. Definitely afternoon. "What brings you here on a day off? Haven't seen enough of me this week?"

"Dad and I went for a walk in Manito Park this morning, so I was in the neighborhood. The flower beds in the Duncan Gardens are newly planted. The conservatory is bustling with visitors. You wouldn't even guess a grisly murder took place there a year ago," she said, referring to the death of the head gardener, the first case the two detectives had solved together.

"I'll be seeing Beau later today. I hope to give him an update on the search warrant for Tom's Taxidermy financial records. Seems like it's taking awhile."

"Yes, it is," replied Rex. "Judge Marconi has been tied up with a large court caseload. He did approve it though. The warrant arrived Friday while you were training wildlife officers how to defend themselves. We have warrants for the Korean Market, Tofucious and Varmint Outfitters, too. I'd like to accompany the wildlife officers when they serve the warrants."

"I'm sure Beau would be pleased with an added show of force," said Ivy. "You and I are really getting to use that interagency training we took in Seattle, aren't we?" Before Rex could inject an answer, she added, "I had fun helping the young wildlife officers with the self-defense training last week. The department's trying to diversify the workforce so there's a lot of female recruits."

So long as they aren't trying to recruit Ivy, thought Rex, gratingly.

"Did you stop by the hospital this morning?" the junior detective asked.

"Yes, Scout's still in a coma. His dad and Chief Blueblood were with him. It's been over a month now. The family isn't ready to give up yet, but it's taking a toll on the chief. We need to make some progress on this case."

Chapter 22

POACHED

First Week in June

Later that week, Rex and Ivy sat across a table from Hentan and Lear at the Spokane County Jail. Wildlife Officer Beau Hunter and his partner Teddy Bruin had hauled the two outlaw musicians in after discovering them beside their pickup on a logging road miles from town. The pickup had a flat tire and the ex-cons didn't have a spare. They didn't have a hunting license, either. The ratty tarp in the truck bed didn't quite cover the bear carcass or the guns. With no hunting permits and in illegal possession of guns, the two Siberian Slayers were sitting ducks. They agreed to talk in exchange for leniency and a ride back to town.

The wildlife officers had proposed to meet Rex and Ivy to assist with questioning. Sheriff Wyatt had extended an invitation to host the gathering.

"Detectives, meet Bruno Hentan and Russ Lear," said Teddy Bruin. "They've offered to tell us what they know about bear trafficking in the area. It could shed some light on the Darkfoot case."

"Wait a minute. We ain't exactly offering. We didn't have no choice," griped Hentan. "And we're talking about killing bears, not people. There's a big difference."

"Well, let's start with you telling us what you know about hunting and selling bear," suggested Bruin.

Lear remained quiet while Hentan recounted how they grew up hunting in the area. At first it was just for sport and meat. It wasn't until after they were released from prison and low on cash that they learned Tom Cathartes paid big money for bear. He paid $1,500 - $2,000 per animal. But since last fall, he'd cut the payout down to $750 to $1,000 a bear.

"When we bitched, he said that was the best he could do. He was getting squeezed," Hentan said.

"What do you mean – squeezed?" Beau Hunter asked.

"Said there was a new buyer in town. The new guy paid Tom less, so he had to pay us less."

"What was Cathartes selling and why did he accept less money for it?" asked Rex.

"He was selling to the Koreans at the market in Hillyard. They took the meat and organs, sometimes the paws. I could sorta understand the meat, but the rest of that shit – I dunno, man. Some people have weird taste," Hentan commented.

No kidding, thought Rex while eyeing the two miscreants.

"So, who is Cathartes selling to now?" asked Teddy Bruin.

"Don't know. Says he can't talk. Too dangerous. But whoever it is, they got a big operation. More bears are being hauled outta the woods now and it's happening all over the Northwest," said Hentan.

"What about Danny Darkfoot? Or Scout Blueblood? Were either of them involved with bear trafficking?" Rex asked.

"I said I don't know nuthin about nobody getting killed and I already told you more'n I shoulda." Hentan hunched down and scowled at the detective.

"Hey," interceded Ivy in a calm, quiet voice. "We're just trying to determine if Danny or Scout were mixed up with the bear traffickers somehow."

"Danny did a lot of dumb shit with drugs, but he was straight when it came to hunting. Some sorta Indian shit – honor the animals or something outta respect for the elders. He guided for Varmint Outfitters, but something happened last fall. Done a couple more hunts then started layin' low."

"What happened?" Rex asked.

"Can't say."

"Can't, or won't?" Rex pressed.

"What about Scout?" asked Ivy, to avert a potential flare-up.

"Don't know. Scout's that guy that worked for Tom, right? Friend of Danny's? Hard to see how he wouldn't know something's going down, being in the taxidermy shop and all. Never talked with neither of 'em. You gotta talk to Tom if you want more info."

Rex guessed as much. Trouble was, Cathartes disappeared within hours of his financial records being seized. "Cathartes wasn't at the taxidermy shop, and we haven't found him at home. Where would we find him?" The detective asked, wondering if anyone else might disappear.

"Probably hiding or dead," Lear muttered quietly, his eyes downcast.

Everyone else at the table stared at him.

Rex spoke first, "What do you mean by that?"

But neither Lear nor Hentan would say any more. The conversation was finished. The two poachers were returned to their cells.

Rex turned to Bruin and Hunter. "Did you learn anything from Cathartes' financial records?"

"Yeah. He had a second set of books, the 'official' business records and the ones he really used to keep track of his money," responded Officer Bruin. "He was trafficking all right. Those two criminals were telling the truth. Up until last fall, he made payments for gall bladders and bile. Sometimes, he'd pay for other parts too, but mostly bile and bladders."

"Any names of who he was paying, or who was paying him?" questioned Rex.

"That's where the notes become cryptic," Bruin replied. "Looks like he used a combination of initials and graphics instead of names. It might take awhile to decipher."

"We've posted an APB looking for Cathartes," Hunter added.

It was late afternoon by the time Rex and Ivy returned to the precinct. Chief Blueblood called Rex into his office, where his brother, Tribal Chief Andy Blueblood, sat waiting.

"Winnie Milne wanted me to pass along a message to you," Andy said after they greeted each other. "She's had another dream. You were in this one," he said, looking at Rex and pausing to watch the detective's reaction.

Rex recalled the elderly lady's vivid account of a large bear attacking her grandson Danny Darkfoot, who later turned up murdered. But she barely knew Rex. How and why would she dream about him? He looked puzzled.

"Winnie dreamed you were lost in a snowstorm. You were hurt and calling for help."

Rex waited for more, but Andy was silent. "That's the dream? That's all?"

"That's it," said Andy. "She was concerned about you. Winnie is an elder. Her dreams have proven true in the past and should be taken seriously."

"But it's June," said Rex. "Almost summer. Time for flowers, not snow. Or, does she have premonitions months in advance?"

"Hard to say. The snow could be representative of something else, or it could be an early warning."

"Okay. Thanks," said Rex, wondering if he would remember to be wary six months from now. And be wary of what? His preferred snowy day activity consisted of a hot beverage, a good book and a warm fire.

Chapter 23

AN INVITATION

Second Week of June

By the time Rex had finished his second cup of cappuccino at the precinct office the next morning, three phone messages waited for him. One was from Teddy Bruin, another from Sheriff Wyatt and a third from Molly Murrow. He called Molly back first.

"Hey, Handsome," Molly's honey-smooth voice answered. "I haven't heard from you for awhile."

Handsome? He reminded himself she used caller ID. "Sorry about that. The Danny Darkfoot case has occupied my mind lately. Progress is slow. People keep disappearing. Anyway, you called here. What can I do for you?"

"I was hoping you might have an update on the case. Any persons of interest? Anything we can report on the morning news yet?"

Confirming the discovery of Danny Darkfoot's van was the last information Rex had shared with the media. And Molly had helped with getting the word out about the van, which led to its discovery. He felt obligated to repay the favor. His many years of knowing Molly personally and working with her professionally led him to trust her.

"I don't want the story to get ahead of the investigation," Rex said, "but if you can sit on the information for a bit, I may be able to give you a bigger story than Danny Darkfoot's murder." He went on to explain that Danny's demise might be tied up in a regional black bear poaching and trafficking operation and that he and Ivy were working with the Department of Fish and Wildlife. "We've run into a dead-end getting information out of two key suspects – Boone Crockett and Tom Cathartes. In fact, Cathartes is missing."

"You don't think he's been killed too, do you?"

"It's always a possibility. But he did vanish right after we started digging into his finances, so maybe he wanted to disappear. In your years of investigative reporting, did you ever discover any dirt on Boone Crocket with Varmint Outfitters or Tom Cathartes, owner of Tom's Taxidermy?" Rex inquired.

"No, but I'll ask around," offered Molly. "I have an idea."

After thanking Molly and hanging up, Rex rang Teddy Bruin. "Any word on Cathartes whereabouts?" he asked the wildlife officer.

"Not yet. But we've received a tip that a major shipment of gallbladders will pass through the Seattle Port this month. The FBI invited me to be there when the U.S. Customs and Border Protection intercept the goods. They're hoping the gallbladders can be tied to the case we've been building here in the Spokane area. The U.S. Fish and Wildlife will be there, too. It will be a real multi-agency bust. Want to join me? The agency is flying me over in a private plane so I can check out a suspected large poaching operation in the North Cascades on the way over to the Port."

Rex's curiosity overcame his reluctance for multi-agency work. He still wasn't sure the Darkfoot and Blueblood cases were related to smuggling bear parts, but it was the only slim lead he had. Would Chief Blueblood agree to what could be a wild goose – or bear – chase when he still hadn't found out who had assaulted the chief's nephew? He promised to get back to Officer Bruin later that day.

"One slight detail, are you okay with flying in a small plane, Detective?" Bruin asked.

It wouldn't be the first time Rex flew in a small plane. Fortunately, his fascination with aerial views overpowered any anxiety. Somehow flying around in a plane looking for criminals seemed more glamorous than driving around the back streets of Spokane in the Crown Vic. Even better, he would miss washing the fire trucks that weekend.

The Port visit was scheduled for June 15. He would be over and back in a day and home in time to celebrate the literary Bloomsday on June 16. Having just finished James Joyce's *Ulysses*, he planned to walk about town that day and raise a toast in his local pub, O'Donovan's, where he had a date with Molly.

Rex signed off with Officer Bruin and called Sheriff Wyatt.

Sheriff Annie Wyatt didn't have any updates on Catharte's location, but she had some surprising news. "I did more checking on that hunting accident you asked about," she said. "The Korean client that died – turns out he was the brother of the owner of the Korean Market and Tofucious Restaurant."

Chapter 24

Flyboys and Poachers

Friday, Mid-June

Rex met Officer Teddy Bruin at the Bomber Cafe early Friday morning. The 24-hour cafe was a favorite hangout of pilots who flew out of next-door Flyboy Field, a nearby general aviation relief airport at the eastern edge of Spokane. More than 150 aircraft called the two-runway airport with adjacent river landings home.

Over a strong cup of black coffee bound to keep a pilot flying for hours, Rex looked around the cafe admiringly. Black and white photos of WWII fighter planes and bombers covered the walls. Model planes hung from Art Deco light fixtures and a propeller framed a large clock above the doorway. Stacks of colorful Fiesta plates and pitchers lined shelves on the wall behind a curved, red, laminate countertop.

Even though it was a few minutes after five in the morning, Planet Claire played on the jukebox as Officer Bruin came through the door and crossed the black and white tiled floor to where Rex sat waiting in a red, high-backed booth. The waitress brought them menus and refilled Rex's coffee.

"The special looks good," said Officer Bruin, eying the description of a three-egg, sausage, onion and green pepper omelet with a sky-high pile of hash browns.

Rex nodded but searched for lighter fare. He settled on a veggie scramble. A big platter of food might be fine for his companion, who looked like a 300-pound linebacker, but Rex was thinking about the weight capacity of a small plane. He began to wonder just how much it could carry.

He needn't have worried. The Cessna 182 Skylane boasted four seats and was known as a workhorse that could carry a full load of fuel, passengers, and cargo.

They found the aircraft parked near the runway at Flyboy Field. Pilot Will Bright had already fueled the pearl-colored plane with the name Orville scrawled in navy blue lettering on the side. Because fuel cost less in Spokane than in the expensive Seattle area, he had filled both tanks. It should be plenty for getting across the state and back. He did a final pre-flight check with the mechanic and then waved Rex and Teddy over to the Cessna.

"Ever fly in a small plane before?" Bright asked Rex after Bruin introduced them. Teddy Bruin had flown with Bright many times during other jobs contracted with the Department of Fish and Wildlife.

Rex assured the pilot that he had flown in small planes before but not routinely, like Bruin did. He would sit in back while Teddy sat up front with Bright to help balance the plane's weight. Bright gave them a cursory overview of the plane and safety instructions.

"We'll be using flight following," said Bright. "That means I'll be communicating with Air Traffic Control and monitoring other plane communications continuously. When I need to concentrate on radio traffic, I'll put my hand up to signal for you to be quiet. Here. You'll want to wear these noise-canceling headphones," he said, handing them each a pair. "We'll still be able to hear each other, but Orville can be loud. Oh, and keep your seat belts on at all times.

"Orville and I have an excellent safety record. We've always returned our passengers home safely and I intend to keep that record," Bright declared.

Rex was thankful for that. He stowed his satchel in a baggage area behind the rear seats. He always carried standard equipment like a camera and notepad, but because they were traveling to Seattle, he also brought a jacket. And he never left town without a packed lunch and a thermos of coffee.

The morning promised a good day for flying – clear skies and a low chance, if any, for inclement weather. Bright did warn, though, there was a chance a storm could move in that evening, so they needed to stick to a tight schedule.

They planned to circle over a reported hunting camp in a clearing in the North Cascades during the morning hours. Reports of multiple bear carcasses rotting in the woods up the Lost River Drainage caused the Department of Fish and Wildlife to expand its investigation westward to the eastern slopes of the Cascade Mountains. Officer Bruin intended to identify the location of the camp and use a good set of binoculars for an initial assessment before sending agents in on the ground.

After searching for the camp, the pilot would take them to King County Airport where FBI Agent Ursula Maidger was scheduled to pick up Rex and Teddy Bruin and drive them to the Port of Seattle. There, they planned to join the rest of the federal law enforcement agents investigating the trafficking operation. At some point during the day, Rex hoped to eat the caprese sandwich and fruit he had packed.

As the pilot did a final check of the instruments, the detective glanced at his phone for any last-minute messages from Ivy before switching his phone to airplane mode. She and Beau Hunter would continue the search for Tom Cathartes and follow-up on any other leads related to the Darkfoot and Blueblood cases while he was out of town. No messages. Rex reminded himself he would be gone only for the day.

They took off at 6:30 a.m. The plane climbed easily into the morning air, the propeller and engine making reassuring vibrations and sounds. Below him, Rex could see the Spokane River winding through the middle of the city, sunlight already gleaming off the water and surrounding buildings. The river flowed under TJ Meenach Bridge, near where Danny's body was found. It then coursed through Riverside State Park, where towers of basalt rose from the water's depths, before aiming northward to empty into the mighty Columbia River. Pine trees soon gave way to farmland, a quilt of green and brown fields. Aerial perspectives always enthralled Rex.

At 8,500 feet, the plane settled into a level flight. The consistent hum of the engine allowed Rex to relax into deep thought as he studied the landscape below. He possessed a fondness for maps and enjoyed the challenge of identifying the geographical features and towns in view. From the air, he could see the scars of the Great Missoula Floods that scoured the

Eastern Washington scablands. The aerial evidence had solved a geographical mystery about the scablands' formation. Now if only he could solve the human mystery nagging his mind.

"We're nearing the area where the camp is purported to be," Teddy Bruin announced, as they neared the eastern slopes of the Cascade Mountain Range.

Rex was startled out of his thoughts. The pilot asked and was given permission by Air Traffic Control to reduce altitude. Officer Bruin pulled out his binoculars and surveyed the forest below.

"Can we get any lower?" Bruin asked. "I see something near the small lake on our right. It might just be water, but the reflection looks different."

By now, Rex had pulled out his binoculars and joined the search. Sure enough. There. Partially covered with camouflage netting, sat a dark pickup truck. A mirror must have reflected the sunlight. Closer inspection revealed a sophisticated camp site concealed by netting and thick foliage. No road led to the camp. It looked like whoever was using the camp drove off-road to the site from a Forest Service road a few miles distant. The camp sat a stone's throw from a basalt cliff.

"Those dirtbags!" exclaimed Bruin. "They didn't even take entire animals." He pointed to an area below the cliff where a murder of crows and a couple of coyotes fed on a pile of bear carcasses. "Looks like they were so focused on getting the organs out, they just left everything else. Damn!"

There didn't appear to be any human activity at the camp at the moment. All was quiet. After snapping incriminating photographs and noting the GPS location, Bruin instructed Bright to resume their flight to the King County Airport. The evidence gathered would be valuable for the poaching and trafficking case the wildlife department was building.

As Rex took a last look through his binoculars, he thought he saw movement near the partially covered truck. Had they been spotted?

Chapter 25

A MULTI-AGENCY APPROACH

Friday, Afternoon

Rex was still thinking about the bear camp when he, Officer Teddy Bruin and FBI Special Agent Ursula Maidger pulled into the parking area at the Port of Seattle. The Port's Police Chief and two canine U.S. Customs and Border Protection officers with their dogs led Rex and his colleagues to the Customs and Border Protection office at Terminal 18.

The Port bustled with activity. A crane operator maneuvered a large orange Gantry Crane as it picked up 40-foot-long, steel containers and stacked them on a ship the length of three football fields. Longshoremen loaded and unloaded containers on and off rail cars and trucks. Yard hostlers, specialized semi-trucks for moving containers, scurried around the terminal like ants on an anthill. Trucks honked and lined up to unload their cargo. Seagulls squawked and flew overhead looking for scraps from longshoremen on their lunch break.

Don't even think about it, Rex telepathically warned a seagull swooping toward him like a B-52 ready to drop its payload.

Slightly over a month had passed since he and Ivy toured the Port as part of the interagency training. And now here he was meeting with agents and officers from the Federal Bureau of Investigation, state and federal wildlife agencies and the U.S. Customs and Border Protection as part of an international wildlife trafficking investigation. Was he any closer to solving Danny Darkfoot's murder and the assault of Scout Blueblood?

Inside the Customs and Border Protection Office, Kay Neine, area port director, welcomed the agency representatives and offered them beverages and grilled salmon sandwiches with a side of pasta salad for lunch. This close to the coast, Rex wasn't going to turn down seafood. The caprese sandwich could keep in his satchel for later.

Neine explained that CBP officers were using a VACIS machine to scan the intermodal containers that had arrived at the terminal by truck that morning. Rex remembered the VACIS machine from his tour of the port. The VACIS machine, or vehicle and cargo inspection system, used gamma rays to examine the interior of containers to detect explosives, weapons, drugs, and even people. The CBP officers would then compare the contents of the container with the cargo listed on a ship's manifest.

"Additionally, we have CBP canines sniffing the cabs of every truck and vehicle entering the terminal," said Neine. "If bear parts are moving through the terminal today, we'll find them."

It was a big case. State and federal wildlife officers had been investigating bear poaching operations for the past two years. What once seemed like a few small, separate operations in the northwest states grew into a much larger, coordinated network of poaching and trafficking. Information collected by Teddy Bruin and the Fish and Wildlife Department's Spokane Office played a major role in the case. As the case extended across state lines, the FBI joined the hunt. Today, the agencies were zeroing in on the international link.

Officer Bruin informed the others about the hunting site and bear carcasses he and Rex observed that morning while flying over the Cascades. The poachers were getting greedier and bolder.

After finishing his sandwich and a handful of cookies, Bruin turned to Rex. "Hey Begonia, are you going to finish that last sandwich?" he asked, nodding his head toward a tray on the table in front of Rex. A lonely sandwich was all that remained on the tray.

"It's all yours," said Rex, who was savoring an after-lunch coffee and was thankful not to be responsible for feeding the much larger wildlife officer. He passed the tray to the burly Bruin.

Area Port Director Neine's phone buzzed. "This could be the shipment we're expecting," she said after ending the call. "Canine officers checking a container of perfume bottles grew suspicious when a bottle broke and sent the dogs into a frenzy. I'd like a couple of wildlife officers to head over to the south container yard and check it out. Meanwhile, I'll put a hold on the cargo and have the truck driver detained."

Teddy Bruin and a federal agent volunteered. Rex offered to accompany them. Officer Bruin, having worked trafficking cases before, knew what to look for when examining the shipments.

When they arrived at the container yard, a young Customs officer, Ben Force, handed him a dark-colored bottle with a gold cap and the words "Eau du Bare" on the side. Bruin opened it and took a whiff. "Whew! That's Bare all right – bear bile!"

"No wonder the dogs went crazy," said Officer Force. "They acted like they'd treed a grizzly."

"Bear bile is used in traditional medicines in Asian countries around the world," Bruin explained to the CBP officer. "Where was this shipment headed?"

"We ran the ship's manifest through the Automated Export System. Said the container is destined for Moscow, Russia," the Customs officer answered. "I thought you said this stuff's used in Asian medicines?"

"It is. But the trafficking of bear parts is widespread," explained U.S. Fish and Wildlife Officer Mel Woods. "Bears are often killed in one country and their parts are exported and often re-exported to other countries. This bile was probably meant to go from Russia to South Korea or China."

"What else is in here?" asked Rex, pulling a bottle out of a box taken from the shipping container.

Most of the cargo appeared to be processed fruits and vegetables, including bottles of Northwest wines and liquors.

"Someone's got fine taste," said Rex looking at the label of well-aged brandy.

"Maybe. But check this out," Officer Force said, handing Rex another bottle. "We found 120 of these bottles. They were in boxes of apple brandy, but the boxes looked slightly different than the others."

Rex unscrewed the lid and sniffed. "Vodka?!"

And what was that at the bottom of the bottle? It looked like a gray glob.

"Gallbladders!" exclaimed Bruin. "They're shipping gallbladders inside bottles of alcohol."

"This is a big enough operation we can justify the expense of DNA tracing," U.S. Fish and Wildlife Officer Woods explained. "Let's get samples sent to our forensics lab in Ashland, Oregon. We might be able to connect the shipment with the cases you've been working on in Eastern Washington," she said to Bruin.

While the CBP officers impounded the cargo and packaged samples for shipping to the lab, Rex and the wildlife officers returned to the Customs and Border Protection office to brief FBI Agent Ursula Maidger, the Port of Seattle Police Chief and Area Port Director Kay Neine. Neine shared that the cargo manifest listed the Russian company Misha as owner of the shipment. It appeared to be a shell company. The FBI would investigate who owned the company.

Danny Darkfoot and Scout Blueblood grew up on the Spokane Indian Reservation in rural Eastern Washington. Could they have become involved in a big, international, illegal smuggling operation, wondered Rex. While the wildlife officers were describing the bile and gallbladder shipment to the others, he received a text from Ivy. Scout Blueblood had come out of the coma and doctors would let people talk with him soon. Also, she and Beau Hunter had picked up Tom Cathartes. "Update U when U R back," she had written. This was welcome news!

Rex looked at his Bulgari watch. While he and Bruin were at the Port of Seattle, pilot Will Bright had spent the day attending to other business. Rex and his wildlife colleague were due to meet Bright back at the King County Airport in less than an hour, traffic permitting. The flight would take another hour. With luck, the detective could be back at the office 15 minutes before Ivy left for the day.

By the time Ursula Maidger dropped Officer Bruin and Rex off at the airport, Rex was reconsidering his cynical views of interagency law enforcement. It had been a successful day, and with Scout emerging from the coma, they would solve his assault case soon.

Chapter 26

A STORM BUILDS

June 15, Late Afternoon

"We have to get in the air quickly," Bright explained, as the detective and wildlife officer climbed aboard the Cessna. They had arrived at the airport late after getting stuck in traffic, which Seattle was now more famous for than rain. "There's been a change in the weather forecast and a storm is moving in quicker than anticipated. If we leave immediately, we should be able to outrun it. We'll have the wind at our tail."

The skies no longer looked clear. Off to the West, clouds began to grow higher and darker. It was unusual, but not unheard of, to have a storm spring up this time of the year. Rex didn't need a reminder to tighten his seat belt and keep quiet.

Will Bright was talking to Air Traffic Control. They would fly back to Spokane using Instrument Flight Rules and Bright was requesting clearance for takeoff. As they climbed into the sky, Rex looked down at the cars on I-5, sitting as if in a parking lot. He was thankful to no longer be among them. He hoped his and Bruin's earlier traffic delay would not prove detrimental.

The steady ascent and normal engine noises reassured Rex as the plane leveled at 9,000 feet in preparation for crossing the Cascades. He could see the peaks rising like a fortress wall to separate Washington into distinct geographical regions. A heavy snowpack this year meant anything above 4,500 feet was blanketed in white still. Even now, in mid-June, the higher elevations could receive snow. They should have visibility as long as they stayed ahead of the storm. And once they crossed the mountains to the drier side of the state, their chances for clear skies would improve.

As exciting as it was to participate in a multi-agency, international trafficking case and drink specialty espressos in Seattle, Rex felt a longing to be home. He had his own case to wrap up now that he could talk with Scout Blueblood. And maybe he would celebrate when meeting Molly Murrow for lunch the next day. A sputtering sound jolted Rex out of his thoughts.

Will Bright was talking rapidly with Air Traffic Control. He was saying something about the fuel. Then, "Mayday! Mayday!"

Rex braced for the inevitable.

Chapter 27

MAYDAY!

June 15, Late at Night

"I've got bad news," Ivy heard Chief Blueblood say when she picked up her phone. She rubbed her eyes and looked at the time. Less than an hour had passed since she went to bed. She wasn't expected at the office for at least ten hours. But then this wasn't a nine-to-five job, was it?

"The plane with Rex and Teddy Bruin went down in the Cascade Mountains," the chief continued. "Last contact was when the pilot notified Air Traffic Control that they had an emergency. ATC has the plane's GPS transponder's location. Also, the plane's emergency locator beacon triggered the SARSAT system. That's a search and rescue system aided by satellite. So we know where they are. The plane is in the Lost Wilderness."

"Oh no!" Ivy gasped, fully awake now. "Are there any survivors?" She had been working with Rex for only a little over two years, but during that time the curmudgeonly senior detective had grown on her. She couldn't imagine crime-fighting without her mentor and partner.

"We don't know yet," answered the chief. "The Chelan County Sheriff sent out a Search and Rescue Team based on the signal from the locator beacon. But a snowstorm is preventing any aerial assistance. It's hampering the Search and Rescue Team too.

"It wasn't the storm that caused the crash," Chief Blueblood added quietly.

"What?!"

"During the final conversation between the pilot and Air Traffic Control, the pilot indicated he thought something was wrong with the fuel line, like maybe someone had tampered with the fuel," said the chief.

"That would mean someone wanted to kill Rex or Teddy Bruin!" exclaimed Ivy.

"Or, the pilot," the chief reminded her. "But yes, it seems someone didn't want them returning to Spokane." He paused while they both grappled with the reality of that statement. The chief broke the silence. "Do you think there's any correlation between this and the poaching and trafficking case you two are helping the wildlife department with?"

Ivy thought about it. Beau Hunter had arrested the taxidermist Tom Cathartes for his involvement in illegal trafficking of bear parts. After the two separate business accounts were discovered, Cathartes had admitted paying poachers for bear parts, which he then sold on the black market for thousands of dollars in profit. He had offered to cooperate with authorities in return for protection. According to Cathartes, his most recent buyer ruthlessly took over the trafficking operation in the Northwest and had been extorting the taxidermist for lower prices. As the wildlife officers closed in on the operation, Cathartes had feared for his life. He didn't know the whereabouts of the new buyer. And he swore he didn't know anything about Danny Darkfoot's demise.

"It's possible Chief," answered Ivy. "Has anyone tried calling Rex? If Rex and Teddy Bruin are alive and there is a connection to the trafficking case, we need to find them before someone else does."

"The phone's just going to voicemail. He probably had it on airplane mode," said Blueblood. "If he could, he would have called out on the phone. Hang on. I'm getting a call from the Chelan County Sheriff's office."

As Ivy waited on hold, her mind raced. What were the chances that Rex was still alive? What did she know about the Lost Wilderness Area? What could she do to help? She wanted to call Beau and find out what he might have heard from his agency.

Chief Blueblood came back on the line. "More bad news, I'm afraid. The search and rescue operation has been called off until the storm subsides. It's too dangerous to send out a team."

"Chief, they could be alive. Alive and injured! The difference of a few hours might mean the difference between life and death. I'll call Beau. He's experienced in backcountry travel. We can search for them. Will you grant me time off?" She hoped Beau would agree to her crazy idea.

Silence. Then, "I can't let you two go alone. Let me round up some reinforcements and meet you at the office in an hour," said the chief.

As Ivy quickly packed for a wilderness excursion, she listened to the 11 o'clock news on KRUM-TV. Molly Murrow was reporting that local Detective Rex Begonia and Wildlife Officer Teddy Bruin were missing and that the plane they were in crashed in the Cascade Mountains earlier that evening. Was it Ivy's imagination, or did Molly's voice sound like she was straining to stay composed?

Shortly after midnight, Ivy, Beau Hunter, Sergeant Phil O'Dendren, and Officer Scott "Hollywood" Pine headed west in a Spokane Police Ford Explorer into the dark night. Chief Blueblood had authorized official time and use of department equipment. And, in an act of interagency cooperation, Fire Chief Billy Blaize and Firefighter Hal Bernhardt joined the search.

Chapter 28

BLOOMSDAY ONCE MORE

June 16, Early Morning

Rex woke. His head ached. His shoulder screamed in pain. He shuddered from the cold. Slowly he realized where he was. He could smell moist, cold air. And his trained nose smelled blood. He looked around in the fading darkness. Snow fell lightly outside. A couple of fresh inches had accumulated. The luminescence from his watch face showed it was 4:48 a.m. on June 16. Bloomsday. He should be celebrating all things James Joyce today. He had a lunch date with Molly at O'Donovan's Irish Pub in Spokane.

Instead, he was in the Cessna, but it was no longer in the air. It lay still, the engine quiet. The last thing he remembered was the pilot declaring an emergency with Air Traffic Control and that they were going down. Thankfully, nothing seemed broken. With a sharp stab of pain to his shoulder, Rex stiffly maneuvered to where he could get a better view of his companions. Dark red blood covered Will Bright's face and his eyes, staring like glass marbles, reflected only emptiness. As gruesome as the sight looked, Rex had seen far worse during his career as a homicide detective. Blood trickled down Teddy Bruin's face, also. His eyes were closed. A faint sound of breathing gave Rex hope.

After struggling to extricate himself from the wreckage, the detective limped forward and pried open the passenger door. Rex groaned with the effort.

Then Bruin groaned.

"Wait. Was that me or you?" asked Rex.

"Help," wheezed the wildlife officer. "My arm."

"Okay big guy, let's take a look." Rex attempted to sound cheerful as he pulled aside part of the instrument panel that had smashed against Bruin's arm. He cut the man's jacket sleeve with his Swiss Army knife. "Here, can you hold this with your other hand? Just press it against the wound," he said handing Teddy the folded-up sleeve.

"How's Will?"

"Dead. I'm surprised we're alive."

Further inspection revealed a cut on Bruin's head, broken arm and ribs, and a sprained ankle. The front of the plane, where Bright and Bruin sat, had taken the bulk of the impact. Rex pulled the pilot's emergency box out of the plane and found a first aid kit. "Score!" he exclaimed, opening a bottle of ibuprofen, downing two pills and then handing two more to his colleague.

Despite his aching shoulder, Rex clumsily managed to bandage up his companion's cuts. Then, he wrapped Bruin's chest and ankle and made a sling for the man's arm by cutting up a seat belt. The detective gave his colleague some water and pulled an emergency blanket over him to keep the wildlife officer warm. Rex would have to rely on adrenalin and ibuprofen to control his own pain.

"How are you feeling? Will you be okay for a bit? I'm going to hike up to higher ground and try to get a signal on my phone." Rex had already tried the plane's radio with no luck. Hopefully, the SARSAT system picked up a signal from the downed plane and a rescue team was already on the way. He didn't want to count on it though.

"I feel like a mummy. Where'd you learn to wrap like that? I just wish I could be more help to you," ruefully admitted Bruin, as he watched Rex pull items out of the emergency kit – flares, trail mix, lightweight tarp and more.

Rex activated a personal locator beacon from the emergency kit. Then, remembering what was in his own satchel, he withdrew the caprese sandwich and gave Bruin half. "Glad I saved this – real food. And even better..." He pulled out a thermos and poured a capful of hot, dark roast coffee. It was just what he needed. The aroma alone began to revive and warm him.

The storm had passed during the night, but visibility hadn't improved with the coming of day. The snow began to dissipate, leaving heavy, low clouds around the surrounding peaks while cold moisture chilled the air. Rex reached again into his satchel and pulled out a rain jacket – a must for any Seattle visit. And there at the bottom of his bag he found the emergency survival handbook Ivy had given him.

He scanned through the pages: "...tools to survive... Self-reliance is survival... you stand an excellent chance of being rescued before dying of starvation..." Well now that's reassuring, Rex thought, until he remembered Bruin's appetite. The center of the handbook contained a reflective, silver centerfold to use as a signaling device. If only the fog would lift.

Rex handed Bruin the reflective centerfold and the handheld radio. "Here, you can admire my bandaging job in the mirror, but if a plane flies overhead, signal it or try to get through on the radio. My phone doesn't have much charge left. I'm going to scramble up that cliff to the ridge line to see if I can get a signal. I won't be gone long."

Stubby, ancient, sub-alpine fir trees had broken the plane's crash landing. The trees obscured part of the plane but weren't tall enough to completely hide it. A few yards to Rex's right, basalt cliffs rose above the tree-lined meadow where the Cessna rested. He shuddered to think what would have happened if they had hit the cliffs. He gave Bright credit for landing in the meadow. It was too short of a landing space to miss the trees though. If it were just a little longer, the pilot might be alive. A couple of hundred yards to his left, the meadow eased toward a cold, mountain lake. He might not have gotten them home, but Will Bright and Orville had landed them in the best location possible, given the circumstances.

Taking his satchel with his thermos and some of the trail mix, Rex slowly navigated a way through the snow-covered rocks toward the ridge. He remembered with dread Winnie Milne's dream of him lost in a snowstorm. Was this the situation she predicted? How did the dream end? He didn't remember hearing the ending. A raven croaking nearby refocused Rex's attention to his immediate surroundings. Periodically, stones from above broke loose and crashed down past him. As he clung to a bushy Sitka alder to remain upright while crossing a steep rockslide, he marveled at the resilience of the plant life in this inhospitable environment. "You can do this too," he told himself.

By tugging on a subalpine fir, bent almost horizontal by decades of wind, the determined detective pulled himself up onto the ridge and collapsed. He lay on the ground catching his breath and feeling gratitude toward the fir, which reminded him of Ivy's bonsai trees back at the office. His phone rang.

He pulled the phone out of his pocket. The signal strength fluctuated between one and two bars. The screen showed Ivy was calling.

"Rex, thank God you're alive!" Ivy shouted when she heard his voice. "You've ... get out of there..."

"Out of where? Where am I?"

"...plane beacon... Sandycove Lake in the Lost Wildern... Listen, Rex. The plane... sabotaged... know where you are. They are... after you..."

The phone died.

Chapter 29

A Search Party

June 16, Early Morning

"He's alive!" Ivy repeated to her companions. She had tried calling Rex's phone every hour since hearing about the crash last night from Chief Blueblood. That was more than seven hours ago. Since then, she and Beau and the others met up at a trailhead in the Okanogan-Wenatchee National Forest. The trail provided the rescue mission's closest starting point, based on the downed plane's locator beacon.

They pulled out and distributed gear, making sure everyone carried a hand-held radio and a personal locator beacon among other items. Not knowing what they would encounter as they headed into the mountains, they brought ropes and climbing gear, which added to their already heavy packs. Ivy's pack included a thermos full of cappuccino with two splashes of Frangelico. Rex was probably in full caffeine withdrawal by now, she thought.

"Let me help you with that," firefighter Hal Bernhardt said to diminutive Ivy as she hefted her 45-pound pack.

Officer Pine chuckled as Ivy glared and curtly turned down the offer for help. When Pine had pulled a prank on Ivy shortly after she joined the police force, she had used a ninja move on him which resulted in him sprawled flat on the ground. No one on the force questioned the strength of the four-foot, ten-inch, junior detective after that.

"We'll follow the trail as far as we can to move quickly. Then, we'll break off and travel cross-country as we get closer to the crash site. At that point, we'll split into groups of two and spread out to cover more territory," directed Beau, who with the most backcountry experience, had been nominated their leader. "Do you all have the site location's coordinates saved in your GPS?"

They did. The group looked like an expedition force about to set off into the wilderness. Ivy was thankful for the satellite and navigation technology that narrowed the group's task. At 3.8 million acres, the Okanogan-Wenatchee National Forest was larger than Connecticut. Thanks to the locator beacon and their GPS units, the small search party had a fighting chance to find the plane and any survivors. Knowing that someone intending harm could be looking for survivors added to the group's sense of urgency.

The sun began to warm the vast landscape, revealing snow-capped peaks and verdant valleys. The early morning quiet bestowed a serenity of place, belying the anxiety Ivy felt. Her stomach churned.

Chief Blaize pulled a box of donuts out of his truck. "I stopped in Leavenworth on the way here. Thought you coppers might need some extra energy to keep up with us firefighters," he said smiling and looking at his friend Sergeant O'Dendren. "They're Bavarian cream-filled. High-quality calories!"

The situation seemed too serious for joking thought Ivy, but she gladly took a donut, realizing that she hadn't eaten any breakfast yet and was about to leave civilization.

Beau brought the group's attention back to the situation at hand. "Okay. Remember. We aren't the only ones looking for survivors. Keep alert for any suspicious characters," he said. "These guys will be armed and dangerous."

Ivy watched Beau with admiration, but she felt heavyhearted. She knew Rex was alive because he had answered his phone. But the conversation was cut off before she could learn if Officer Teddy Bruin or the pilot were alive. Officer Bruin was Beau's colleague. Beau probably felt as strongly about him as she did about Rex. And, she didn't know the condition of any survivors. Likely, the search team would need to help carry them out, or they would need to call in a helicopter. If they found the survivors before the others did.

Ivy carried her 9 mm Glock in a holster beneath the camouflage hunting jacket that Beau had loaned her. The jacket would help her blend into the surroundings he had told her. She wondered how inconspicuous she looked with the sleeves rolled up and the jacket hanging low. She tucked her bright red hair up under a cap and imagined she looked like a twelve-year old hunter, minus the orange vest. This is similar to a hunt, Ivy thought grimly. But was she predator, or prey?

In addition to his semi-automatic pistol, Beau carried a Remington 700 .30-06 rifle with a scope. Sergeant O'Dendren and Chief Blaize also carried high-powered rifles. And they had backup. Weather had postponed the initial search, but now the Chelan County Sheriff pulled together a few of his deputies. They would follow shortly. As soon as the fog lifted, a search plane would join the hunt too.

Despite her Bloomsday training, Ivy strained to keep up with the firefighters, who soon took the lead up the trail. Ivy didn't like to be outpaced. She vowed to add climbing stairs with a backpack to her fitness training. Maybe she would even enter the annual firefighter stair climbing contest.

The group anticipated hiking about five miles before reaching the spot where they planned to split up and leave the trail. They moved quickly and quietly, listening for any unusual sounds in the woods.

Chapter 30

MAKING TRACKS

June 16, Morning

Rex tried calling Ivy. It was no use. His phone battery had died. Who was after him, he wondered. The plane's locator beacon must have alerted the authorities to the crash site. A rescue team must be on the way. But Ivy had said "sabotage" and the alarm in her voice told him the rescue team wasn't the only one searching for him and Bruin.

If Rex were home, he would be enjoying his second cappuccino of the morning. Instead, he pulled out the thermos with day-old coffee and hoped the caffeine would jolt his brain into thinking. He opened the survival handbook. It said to stay put, stay calm and to think. It also said that remaining with a downed plane improved chances of being found and provided shelter – unless there was a danger from spilled fuel or frozen temperatures. It didn't say anything about being tracked by criminals.

Rex assessed his options. He and Bruin could remain with the plane and hope a friendly search team found them before the saboteur did. They could hide near the plane and watch to see who approached – friend or foe. He assumed whoever was after them was armed, but he didn't know how many there were. Also, the meadow and lake didn't offer much cover for hiding. The third option was to hike out of the mountains and hope to reach safety before being discovered. He didn't know whether Bruin could hike with his injuries. Rex hoped so. He preferred that they have some control over their destiny.

Before leaving the ridge, Rex took a long look, studying the landscape. The clouds started to lift and he could see the plane in the meadow below him. Patches of yellow stood out where the early-flowering glacier lilies poked through the melting snow. The turquoise-colored lake lay still in the morning air. He made note of the location of the lake's outlet. Water flowing from the lake would create a stream, which would course downhill. If they were lucky, they could follow the stream down the mountain and eventually emerge from the woods. Maybe he could even find their location on the flight map in the plane. He needed to get back to Teddy Bruin.

By the time the detective arrived back at the plane, Officer Bruin had filled a container with water from the nearby lake and had combed through the plane's scattered debris for anything useful. He was fumbling at stringing up a tarp for shelter.

"Don't get too comfortable," said Rex. He told Bruin about the phone call and was dismayed to learn Teddy's phone was destroyed during the crash. "Can you walk? We won't be on a maintained trail. At least not for awhile."

Bruin, who had spent a career in the woods as a wildlife officer and much of his free time hunting and fishing, was game to give it a go. They both took more ibuprofen in preparation for the ordeal. Before leaving, they covered Bright's body with the tarp and held a moment of silence.

May you find peace in the heavens Will and Orville, thought Rex.

Then, Bruin leaned on a makeshift walking stick he found in the trees and he and Rex headed across the meadow toward the lake. Both men brought their weapons, although Bruin's ability to use his was questionable. The detective carried his satchel loaded with their emergency gear. Ironically, they wanted to be found, yet not found – depending on who was doing the finding.

A long shrill whistle sounded as they reached the outlet of Sandycove Lake. Rex looked around suspiciously.

"No worries, Begonia. It's just a pica, kind of like a marmot but smaller. They're as common in these mountain meadows as marmots are along the Spokane River," Teddy Bruin explained when he saw a startled Rex turn his head with concern toward the sound.

Rex wished he knew who was searching for them. Whoever it was, he suspected, probably had something to do with bear trafficking, poaching, or both. He was grateful for the increasing tree cover and decreasing snow as they descended in elevation. He shifted the satchel to favor his injured shoulder. They moved as quietly as possible while following a narrow game trail through the brush, all the while keeping the stream within hearing distance. Bruin was trying not to slow them down, but Rex silently worried about their pace.

They had traveled an agonizingly slow forty minutes when Bruin stopped to examine a pile of scat on the trail. "Looks like a black bear has been using this trail. It's fresh too."

Rex glanced at the pile. It was dark green with bits of grass in it. "It's probably wishful thinking that the bear's vegetarian," he commented dismally.

"Yeah, black bears are omnivorous. Their scat's usually green in the spring. They're eating a lot of grass when they come out of hibernation. That's when they're hungriest." Bruin wheezed. He examined the ground around the scat. "Here's the tracks," he said, pointing to wide, five-toed indentations with long claw marks. "Looks like a large male."

Rex eyed the prints. He visualized a ravenous 500-pound black bear eyeing an Italian American for lunch while Teddy Bruin examined bear droppings.

"Great. Now we have a saboteur and a large carnivore chasing us," groaned the detective.

"Omnivore. They eat both plant and animal matter," said Bruin.

"It's the eating animals that matter," said Rex, noting that humans were animals. "Let's get moving."

After another hour and no more bear signs, Bruin called a halt. They had descended below the snow line and the trail eased. "I need to rest. My ankle's throbbing. We're close to the stream. I'm going to soak it in the cold water for awhile."

Rex hesitated to stop but he knew if he pushed too hard, his companion might not be able to continue. Besides, he heard a growling. He knew it wasn't the bear. It was his stomach reminding him that he hadn't eaten much since yesterday's lunch. They found a log to sit on near the stream.

After recruiting his companion's help to get his shoe off, Bruin moved to a rock, sat and dipped his unwrapped ankle in the icy water. Rex dug through his satchel for the trail mix. It wasn't pasta but it would have to do.

Soon, the wildlife officer was scratching his legs and swearing. The detective hurried toward him and then stopped when he saw a patch of nettles that Bruin had walked through. His companion might know all about animals, but he needed to learn more about plants – at least the dangerous ones. Stinging nettles, while delicious if cooked, had little hairs that emitted chemicals into skin, causing a stinging sensation and a rash. They could be safely harvested only with gloves.

"Don't scratch. That will make it worse."

"Easy for you to say. It feels like someone's sticking needles in a voodoo doll of me." Large, red bumps covered Bruin's legs.

"Fortunately for you my friend, *Impatiens capensis*, or jewelweed, often grows in moist areas near nettles," he said, as he spotted the elliptical, alternately arranged leaves on the upright stems. The beautiful orange flowers wouldn't bloom for another month, but Rex was in his element when it came to plants. He quickly picked some of the jewelweed, crushed the stems and started wiping the sap on Bruin's legs. As he did so, he felt quite pleased with himself for remembering the information he learned in a class on edible and medicinal plants and taught by Manito Park Head Gardener Toni Fritts. Rex finished by drying and re-wrapping his companion's less swollen, but now itchy and red ankle.

"Thanks. I guess it helps to know something about plants as well as animals out here," wheezed Bruin.

"Well, you can take care of the bears. Here, have some trail mix. It might be the only lunch we get today," offered Rex. "I just wish we knew more about who's looking for us and where they are."

The next moment, they both froze at the sound of a branch snapping in the brush.

Chapter 31

PREDATOR OR PREY

June 16, Late Morning

Four miles from the trailhead, Ivy and her companions reached a trail junction. On an old, wooden trail sign, the name above an arrow pointing to the left read 'Easy Street.'

"Stay to the right," said Beau, after consulting his GPS.

"Look! Footprints," Ivy exclaimed, pointing to indentations in the trail's moist soil.

"They appear fresh," Sergeant O'Dendren added.

Beau brought a finger to his lips to hush them and crouched down to study the tracks. The others followed his example. After a closer examination of the footprints, the group concluded that three people had recently traveled the adjoining trail, which connected to a nearby drainage. The footprints were headed in the same direction as the search group.

"What are the chances the prints belong to Detective Begonia and the others?" whispered Officer Pine.

"I don't think so," Ivy quietly answered. "The tracks are headed in the wrong direction. And Rex probably wore his Ferragamo dress shoes to the meeting at the Port. These prints were made by someone wearing boots."

"Whoever it is, they probably aren't expecting us," said Beau softly. "They probably saw the news about the plane crash and postponed search party. Now, they probably figure they have a chance to find the plane before the authorities do."

"Let's move off the trail and into the woods. We need to be less conspicuous. Stick close to your partner and stay within sight of everyone else, at least for now. Use your radios to keep in contact if we do get separated, but stay as quiet as possible. And keep moving toward the plane. We need to see what happened there."

Keeping his voice low, Sergeant O'Dendren radioed their location and the news about the prints to Chelan County Sheriff Dan Knotts. Then, he and Officer Pine veered off into a stand of Engelmann spruce and larches. Chief Blaize and Hal Bernhardt slipped into the woods on the other side of the trail.

That left Ivy with Beau. It seemed as if they spent more time together at work than dating these days. The pair quickly followed the others into the woods.

They hadn't gone far when Beau stopped. "Those footprints aren't the only fresh markings," he said, showing Ivy new slashes about five-feet high on the trunk of a leaning spruce tree. "Look, that tree over there has similar markings, just older. A bear must regularly pass through here."

Ivy's heart raced faster. Were the occupants of the plane okay? What would Rex do if he encountered a bear? She didn't think he claimed any experience with live bears. He wasn't the camping type.

The trees thinned as she and Beau emerged into a meadow and found the Cessna. The nose was smashed into a small grouping of firs at the meadow's edge. The landing gear and one wing were stripped off and lay scattered among the glacier lilies poking through the melting snow. Surprisingly, much of the plane remained intact, lifting Ivy's hopes.

Chief Blaize and Bernhardt were already at the crash site. So were Sergeant O'Dendren and Officer Pine, who were guarding the site and watching for crooks. But the occupants of the plane were missing. At least two of them were. Chief Blaize pulled the tarp back to expose Will Bright, whose expression was frozen in death and the cold air.

The expression on Beau's face saddened. He knew Bright from many Department of Fish and Wildlife projects and flights into the backcountry. Ivy reached out and held Beau's arm until he pulled himself together.

"Okay, we have to assume Detective Begonia and Officer Bruin are alive. Our priority is to find them and ensure their safety," Beau directed, while forcing his thoughts to focus on the emergency at hand. "Let's see if we can find any clues as to which way they went."

Beau called Sheriff Knotts on the radio to provide an update about the plane's discovery, Bright's body and the missing passengers. They conferred about ordering a helicopter. The fog had cleared and the meadow could provide a suitable landing spot.

Meanwhile, Ivy wandered away from the group. The turquoise lake caught her eye. Rex and Officer Bruin would need water. Maybe she would find a sign of them near the lake.

She was kneeling among the rushes along the shore examining footprints in the mud, when she heard someone approaching.

"Hey, you shouldn't go off by yourself."

Ivy turned and stood. It was Bernhardt. Did he still doubt her abilities? "I'm fine, thanks," she said, a little too brusquely.

"Whoa. Didn't mean to offend," the firefighter replied, raising his hands.

Ivy instantly regretted her curtness. She always felt a need to prove herself and often reacted too quickly. She admitted that it wasn't a good idea to have left the group, and the young firefighter probably would have followed anyone else who wandered away. She began to apologize, "Sor..."

She heard a crack. Bernhardt fell.

Ivy drew her gun and whipped around toward the cliffs from where the sound originated. As she did, a second bullet hit her pack and knocked her into the rushes. She managed to get off a shot before falling.

She was stunned but unhurt. She crawled to Bernhardt. "Are you okay?" she whispered.

"My arm," the firefighter groaned.

Ivy could see he was bleeding. A rivulet of red flowed toward the turquoise lake. She hoped the others had heard the shots and were pursuing the shooter. She pulled off her pack and drew out a first aid kit and extra clothing to wrap the wound. The first aid kit smelled like – coffee and Frangelico!

After cleaning and wrapping the firefighter's wound, Ivy looked in her pack. A brown, wet liquid seeped onto the remaining items in the pack. She held up the thermos. A bullet had pierced the steel container.

Bernhardt sniffed his bandages. "Wow! Saved by a shot of espresso!" he exclaimed.

141

Chief Billy Blaize joined them at the edge of the lake. "You two alright?" Ivy smiled at Bernhardt and then turned to Chief Blaize. "We're okay. Your buddy was grazed in the arm, but I think he'll live." Then she asked, "What happened to the shooter?"

"O'Dendren and Pine went after him," said Blaize. He was inspecting Ivy's treatment on his colleague's arm. "Nice work. You could be an EMT. We might have to recruit you on our firefighting team." He and Ivy helped Bernhardt to stand. The group turned toward the Cessna. Blaize carried their gear and this time, Ivy didn't object to the assistance.

A large group had gathered alongside the plane. Chelan County Sheriff Knotts and the official search party had arrived. The sheriff took command of the situation, which included taking into custody the two thugs that O'Dendren and Pine had captured on the rock cliffs. One of them was hobbling while his friend yelled at him in Russian.

"Shut your mouth, you sap," the taller one glared at his friend.

"Hey!" exclaimed Officer Pine.

Ivy recognized the two brutes from the hunting photos on the wall and in the brochures at Varmint Outfitters.

"Nice shot, Ivy," said Sergeant O'Dendren, who witnessed the shooting incident before chasing after the thugs. "Your maneuver was a bit unorthodox, but you managed to hit this guy in the ankle," he said, handing the taller criminal off to a deputy sheriff. "It slowed them down enough we were able to catch them."

"These crooks are part of a poaching and trafficking ring," Beau explained to Sheriff Knotts. "The Russians have been trafficking black bear parts in the Northwest. They eliminated their Korean competition and consolidated all illegal bear trade in the area. We picked up some of their crew in Spokane and Department of Fish and Wildlife officers are closing in on their camp, just a few miles from here."

"Wait," Ivy said. "We caught two guys but saw three sets of footprints. Where's the third person?"

Chapter 32

THE WIND SHIFTS

June 16, Mid-Day

Rex motioned to Officer Bruin to be silent. He looked around for cover. If they moved quietly and stayed in the brush they might be able to cross the creek where it narrowed, a short distance upstream. On the other side of the stream, large basalt rocks created a fortress bulging outward from the slope. A ledge at the top of the rock outcropping could give them a view of the surrounding area while keeping them hidden behind the basalt and the brushy vegetation.

The detective pointed the spot out to Bruin, who nodded in recognition of the plan. The sound of more movement in the woods behind them motivated the two men to flee. Rex gave the wildlife officer credit. Despite his injuries and his size, Bruin could move stealthily in the woods. They reached the vantage point on the rock ledge and peered around a large basalt boulder.

A few feet from where they had just rested near the water, stood a large black bear. Blood oozed from an injured shoulder and became matted in its fur. The bear huffed and grunted. It lowered its injured body and drank from the stream.

The wind shifted. The bear lifted its head and sniffed.

Rex glanced at Teddy Bruin. Now, it was Bruin's turn to motion to Rex to be still. They waited a few minutes and then glimpsed back toward the stream. The bear was no longer there.

Rex heard a growl. He looked up. There on a ledge twelve feet above them stood the bear glaring down at them.

Chapter 33

CLOSING IN

June 16, Mid-Day

Sheriff Knotts and his deputies controlled the crash site. Reinforcements were called in to help secure the area and remove the plane and Will Bright's body. A helicopter was on the way to retrieve the suspects.

Ivy and the other searchers from Spokane continued the hunt for Rex and Teddy Bruin farther down the trail.

"Over here!" shouted Sergeant O'Dendren. He had discovered shoe prints on a game trail. "It's got to be Rex. Notice the shape of the print. It's a dress shoe, not a boot."

A much larger, second set of prints looked like they could belong to Officer Bruin. "It looks like he might be hobbling and using a stick," remarked Beau, examining the unusual pattern in the soil.

After following the footprints for about one hundred yards, the group came upon another set of tracks. "Black bear," said Beau. "From the size of the prints, I'd guess a male or a large sow."

The group also noticed boot prints. They matched the ones discovered earlier.

The bear prints and the boot prints headed in the same direction as the shoe prints. The searchers quickened their pace. In a few feet, they noticed drops of blood on the trail. The size of the drops increased the further they traveled. They heard a commotion ahead of them in the brush. Now they ran, guns ready.

Chapter 34

A CONFRONTATION

June 16, Mid-Day

The bear stood on its hind legs and roared. It lunged. Rex yelled and dove evasively aside. He tumbled over rocks. He felt like a barrel rider going over Niagara Falls. Fortunately, he didn't fall far. When he looked up, he saw the black bear wrestling a person. The bear growled and bit down on the person in its embrace.

"Teddy!"

"Up here," called Bruin from the ledge. "Try to get a broadside shot at it behind its shoulder!"

Rex ached all over, but he pulled out his handgun and aimed. He waited until he could clearly see the bear's shoulder and the body of the person being mauled. He needed to be quick enough to hit the bear without hitting the person.

A metallic bang rang out. And then a thud.

Chapter 35

AN INJURED BEAR IS A DANGEROUS BEAR

June 16, Mid-Day

The searchers heard the shot. They burst through the brush en masse. A grisly scene greeted them. Bright, wet blood spattered across the rocks and vegetation. It soaked a large swath of the ground and covered the bodies before them. A tangle of bear and man formed a bloody, hairy pile. Another man lie battered and slumped against the rocks.

"Rex!" shouted Ivy and ran to see if he was alive. He was.

"Just need a minute," he whispered. "Check on the other guy."

Ivy walked over to where Beau and Chief Blaize were pulling the bear's bulk off of a short and muscular young man with dark hair and beard. Despite the blood and the claw and teeth marks, Ivy couldn't look away. She recognized him. "Alex. Alex Kamtchatka from Kam's Landscaping!"

It was too late to save Alex Kamtchatka. The bear had torn open the side of his neck, severing the jugular vein.

Sergeant O'Dendren radioed Sheriff Knotts while Ivy and Bernhardt assisted Rex. In addition to numerous scrapes and scratches, the detective's left arm was broken. They wrapped it and made a sling to match Teddy Bruin's right-armed sling.

Chief Blaize and Beau helped Officer Bruin down from the rock ledge. Officer Pine began to secure the area.

The two wildlife officers took a closer look at the bear. "He appears to have been shot in the front and the back of his shoulder," said Beau. "The first shot must have just injured him. Black bears don't typically attack people, but they can be dangerous when injured."

"Well unless one of you shot the bear first, I think he got his man," said Rex. "And am I ever glad he chose Kamtchatka instead of me!" It unsettled

Rex that Kamtchatka managed to sneak up on him and Bruin as closely as he had. The bear may have saved them.

"Your clean-up crew has arrived!" called out Sheriff Knotts, as he and some of his deputies burst onto the scene. "We'll finish up here. I've arranged for a chopper to take you out of the woods, providing you can get back to the meadow okay," he added, looking dubiously at Rex and Officer Bruin with their matching slings, mud-spattered clothes and disheveled appearances.

"Also, I've talked with Chief Blueblood. He wants you back in Spokane tonight. You can go, but I'll need your report on the day's events, once you've recovered."

Beau led the group back to the meadow. Ivy and Blaize carried Rex and Officer Bruin's gear as the two men hobbled behind them. Injuries and an uphill climb slowed the hike back, but at least they were able to stay on the trail and not worry about who or what might be hunting them.

"I'm surprised you knew to follow the stream downhill," Ivy said to Rex as they walked along. I didn't know you were such an outdoorsman."

"Other than sitting outside in my garden, I'm not." Rex reached into his pocket gingerly. He pulled out and handed her the *Pocket Emergency Survival Guide*. "This came in handy."

Ivy smiled.

It wasn't until the long drive home when Ivy could brief Rex on the break in the case that happened while he and Agent Bruin were at the Port of Seattle. With Molly Murrow's help, she and Beau had tracked down Tom Cathartes.

Ivy explained how the taxidermist admitted to paying poachers for bear parts in addition to purchasing legally hunted animals. Originally, he turned around and sold the bear parts to Koreans. The Korean Market and Tofucious Restaurant were the hub for the trafficking. "At that time, only bears were being killed," she said.

"Then the Russians moved in. Remember Varmint Outfitter's hunting trip where the Korean businessman died? Well, it wasn't an accident. He was shot by his guide and the incident was made to look like an accident."

"So Boone Crockett was behind the murder," opined Rex.

"No, he really didn't know the client was murdered," explained Ivy. "Crockett was at the hunting camp but he didn't know the shooting was intentional. He was guilty only of trying to cover up the shooting. He wanted to retain Varmint Outfitters' reputation.

"Alex Kamtchatka was the guide who shot the client. The murder was part of eliminating the Korean competition. Alex hired his buddies at Kam's Landscaping to poach black bear. They worked as hunting guides on the side for Crockett."

"And Danny Darkfoot and Scout Blueblood weren't part of his gang," Rex surmised. "They just knew too much."

"Yeah," finished Ivy. "Alex and his gang killed Danny. They tried to do the same with Scout but were interrupted. As long as Scout was in the hospital, they didn't dare try to kill him. When he could talk, he confirmed Cathartes story.

"That's why Cathartes went missing. He learned that Alex and his gang killed Danny. He feared he might be next."

"You and Beau were busy while I was in Seattle. Good job, Ivy. I'll be glad when we wrap up this case," Rex said wearily. "It's been a long one. And a long day today."

He shut his eyes and let the steady sound of the tires rolling over the pavement put him to sleep. He could nap, for at least three hours, on the ride home.

Chapter 36

END OF DAY TOAST

June 16, Late Evening

"What I don't understand is how Alex Kamtchatka and his buddies knew we were alive and where we were," Rex wondered aloud, while scanning the menu at O'Donovan's Irish Pub.

Despite arriving in Spokane around 9:00 p.m. and the painkillers starting to wear off, Rex was determined to keep his Bloomsday date with Molly Murrow. He had asked Ivy and Beau to drop him off at the pub after arranging to meet Molly there. They checked Officer Bruin into the hospital and then Ivy, Beau and everyone else from Spokane who helped with the search met at the pub, too. O'Dendren argued that even though they were tired from the exhausting day, their hunger took precedence.

"The plane crash was all over the evening news, Sweetie," Molly Murrow explained to Rex. "Anyone watching the news would have known that a famous Spokane homicide detective and a special unit wildlife officer went down with the plane. They would have learned the crash location and that a storm delayed the search and rescue operation, too."

Rex frowned. Molly had inadvertently helped the bad guys.

"Last night, FBI Agent Ursula Maidger arrested the Middendorffs," added Beau. "Turns out, Mikhail Middendorff was the ringleader for the international bear trafficking operation. As a running coach, he traveled with his wife extensively without suspicion. As they went all over the world for running events, he set up the trafficking network. They were in Spokane for the Bloomsday Race. He arranged operations with Alex Kamtchatka and others like him to obtain bear parts. The parts were shipped to Russia to be sold across the border in the Koreas and in China.

"Agent Maidger and her partner arrested the Middendorffs trying to leave Seattle on a red-eye flight. But by that time, Mikhail Middendorff had already contacted Kamtchatka and directed him to find the plane and any survivors. The hunting camp was, unfortunately, located just a few miles from the crash," Beau continued.

"After the FBI agents arrested the Russian coach and his wife, they found a schematic of the Cessna's fuel system and tools in the Russians' pickup. Maidger soon uncovered the story about the sabotaged fuel lines. Middendorff had manipulated the valve that opens the fuel line to the second tank. When the pilot switched to the second fuel tank, the adjusted valve appeared to have operated normally but it didn't open the fuel line at all. The fuel from the first tank just wasn't enough to get the plane back to Spokane."

"Do you know what you would like to order?" asked the friendly young man, Ryan, who had seated them earlier and now come back to check on them.

Rex turned his attention back to the menu. It had been his idea to eat in an Irish pub to celebrate Bloomsday, but he still hoped to find spaghetti on the menu. No spaghetti. The pub did serve an O'Leary's Lasagna though. When it was his turn, he ordered the lasagna. Molly ordered the fish and chips. Sergeant O'Dendren, a regular at the pub, ordered the famous Hooligan and Hanigan sandwich.

When their food arrived, Rex was surprised to find a pile of French fries alongside his lasagna.

O'Dendren laughed when he saw Rex's perplexed look. "Potatoes on the side is what makes it 'O'Leary's Lasagna.' It's not an Irish dish without potatoes. Try them. They're the best fries in town."

Rex had to admit they were. The thick fries, bursting with plenty of potato flavor, contained just the right amount of seasoning. The Irish spuds were so tasty, he decided to be daring and ordered an Irish coffee for dessert.

Jeff, the bartender, brought the coffee to the table. "Hey, aren't you the detective that everybody was looking for in the mountains? The one that went down in the plane?" he asked setting the coffee in front of Rex. After the detective admitted that he was, Jeff and Ryan brought a round of drinks on the house for the entire group.

Detective Rex Begonia looked around the table. Ryan had put the group in the back room, maybe because of the group size, or maybe because they all looked so bedraggled. Either way, Rex was proud of this group of police detectives, wildlife officers, firefighters and, not to forget, a reporter. They had collaborated together to solve a murder case and an international trafficking and poaching case. They had overcome wild weather, fowl felons, and a ring of ruthless Russian racketeers.

Another Irish coffee appeared. Rex wouldn't admit it aloud, but the sweet boozy elixir with a layer of cream could compete with his Italian cappuccino with a splash of Frangelico. Did he see a wink from Sergeant O'Dendren as the coffee was placed in front of Rex?

"I'd like to propose a toast," the senior detective announced and raised his glass, while looking around at the tired but jovial group. "A toast to good friends, a job well done, and completing Bloomsday safely."

"To Bloomsday!"

"Slainte!"

"Cheers!"

"To friends and colleagues!"

When the celebrants finished toasting, Chief Blaize said, "You know me, I hate to end a good party but we have to get up early. We have big day ahead of us tomorrow."

After the group dispersed, Molly offered to drive Rex home. As they left the restaurant, she held his uninjured arm, leaned in and asked sweetly, "Tell me Detective, do you always bring so many chaperones on a date?"

EPILOGUE

June 17, Mid-Morning

"Sorry Rex. I know this is tough on your arm, but we've been putting this day off long enough. The good news is we have lots of volunteers helping," Chief Barney Blueblood said. The chief was giving Rex a ride to Fire Station One, where the Flatfoots were slated to wash fire engines and trucks as per the bet with Fire Chief Blaize.

"I didn't think Blaize would drop the bet. But, how's Scout? Any problems after the coma?"

"Much better, thanks. He's still in the hospital for a day or two while the docs monitor his vitals. He's got a few months of physical therapy ahead of him. My brother Andy is taking some time off of work to help Scout recuperate. It'll be good for them both."

Rex drained the last drops of coffee from his mug as they neared the parking lot of Station One. Three engines, one hook-and-ladder truck and two EMT trucks awaited cleaning. This could take all day, Rex thought disconsolately.

But as the chief and Rex pulled into a parking space on the other side of the trucks, they were greeted by a mob of people with all the equipment needed for a washing party. Beau Hunter helped Ivy and officers Pine, Silva and Hemlock fill buckets with soap and water. Teddy Bruin, newly released from the hospital, sat in a lawn chair and supervised. The whole O'Dendren family, wearing lime green, Bloomsday finisher t-shirts, showed up to help. The firefighters from The Heat team pulled out the fire hoses to spray down the trucks. Even Chief Blaize arrived with coffee and donuts from the Hole-in-One Donut Shop for everyone.

Little Liam O'Dendren was pretending to drive a fire engine and everyone else was getting wet when a KRUM-TV truck pulled up to the scene. Molly Murrow and a camera operator jumped out of the truck.

"Breaking news – I hear the city's police force and firefighters have teamed up to clean up the city," Molly laughed happily and directed viewers' attention to the unfolding caper.

ACKNOWLEDGEMENTS

Blood on Bloomsday is due in large part to the many encouraging readers who asked for more Rex Begonia and Ivy Lizei adventures after enjoying *Murder at Manito*. When introducing Rex and Ivy, I was unsure if others shared my offbeat sense of humor. I'm grateful for the warm response from readers.

My depth of gratitude goes deeper for those readers who gave of their time and effort to give technical and editing advice throughout the process of bringing *Blood on Bloomsday* to fruition. Special thanks goes to Maureen Bieker, Tonie Fitzgerald, Don and Nancy Giese, Jason Givens, Madonna Luers, Jon Newkirk, Woody Myers, and Anne Sittman.